This second edition of *Tolka*
published in Dublin in 2021

Designed by Sarah McCoy
Printed by Creative Design & Print (creativedesignandprint.ie)

ISBN 978-1-739-8226-0-6

Tolka receives financial assistance from the Arts Council.

the arts council
chomhairle ealaíon
funding literature
artscouncil.ie

How They Met Themselves

NIAMH CAMPBELL

I am, in this memory, five years old. I do tap-and-jazz class with my little girlfriends: Lindsey, Fiona, Karen (latterly, in Australia; a yoga teacher; last seen stealing boyfriends at the debs). We return from the hired lodge by the Protestant school – where we dance to 'The Ugly Duckling', 'On the Good Ship Lollipop'; where the air is grainy with dust motes and fragrant of sweet, decaying orchard fruit – via the drained mill pond and contained land-water cataract known to the small town as *the canal*.

We do this every week and the route remains in my memory with strange vividness. On this day I skip ahead of the group and the mother-chaperone to cross a concrete bridge which, if you run through it, produces a tinny echo not unlike the tup-tup-tup of tap and jazz. Spinning out at the end I veer left into a green space, trees and grass, by the edge of the water and almost fall over an elderly man waking up under a tree. He wears a tweed suit and flat cap and looks up at me with a face that is concave – no teeth, I realise later – and causes fear and some additional, dimmer emotion to flute through me like lit gas. I run away and never say a word about it for some reason, never tell a single person, never mention it for years.

And then, at thirty-two, I put this experience in a story. The protagonist, a twenty-something, is confronted by her volatile ex-boyfriend about a crisis pregnancy: she knows she needs to have an abortion and, even though he will not support her either way, he attacks her for her decision. The episode at the canal is repurposed because I have, by now, come to comprehend that dimmer emotion – other than fright – it lit in me:

> *This feeling had the shaming force of one of her earliest memories: returning from tap-and-jazz class with a cloud of girls and one of the mothers, a context which placed her personally at five; they crossed the canal and part of this trip involved crossing a cement bridge. In the memory Nina ran ahead to reach the bridge and trup-trup through it, hearing her footsteps ring like the song,* trup trup a chapaillín. *When she emerged still singing from the bridge she turned sharply into the green space and almost tripped over an elderly man in town style – flat cap and tweed suit – lying under one of the trees.*
>
> *He had no teeth. He raised his sunken face to her in fright.*

The feeling in question, a rich flourish I remember well, was shame, but shame with no obvious application. Why would a five-year-old with no lived experience of addiction feel this at encountering a half-passed-out old man? How could a five-year-old understand that the man was drunk, and probably astray? There is something *Buile Suibhne* to it – the birdman falling out of his tree, the staved face of an apocryphal saint. The scene at five made zero sense, and it makes little sense to me now. This would have been by daylight, at about two o'clock, or perhaps earlier; this would have been 1993, not 1900.

With all I know about composite and symbolic memories, as an adult, now, I have to ask: did it happen at all?

▪

The canal in question led, and leads, to a wide old nineteenth-century street lined with artisans' two-up two-down houses built, originally, for employees of the hosiery factory. A friend of mine, pregnant and sick of renting, recently moved back to our hometown with her partner and bought a house on that very street. My sister and I browse photographs on Daft.ie, some showing a view of the sweeping but volcanically brambled slope to the weir and the wild wasteland that was always wild and covers what was part of the mill pond. The boxy bridge with its stripe of iron showing like a spine through combed concrete remains. The rest of the space is landscaped and serene.

At the top of the nineteenth-century street stands the thin, high old house of my paternal family. There were chickens and a privy once. It would have been inhabited by some or other of my relatives from the time of the factory, when they all worked as toppers and manual finishers of tights and stockings and stays, to 1998, when a distant cousin murdered his wife at the top of the narrow stairs. I knew the house well as a child because I found it entrancing. There was a front room, woodchipped and with one of those pizza-topping-floral carpets, a tiled fireplace built dollishly into the wall; there was the room with a brass-framed bed my great-grandfather slept in until he went into a nursing home; there was the damp peach-horror bathroom tacked to the back of it in the seventies. There was a long, straight garden full of roses my great-grandparents entered into competitions. In the nineties my dad dug out a Japanese maple engulfed by weeds and rehomed it in our garden, where I hope it still grows. This house – all the houses – have been sold.

As a very small child, smaller than five, I had a dream I can remember with the same degree of queasy precocity attached to tap and jazz. In this, I found a severed ear lying on the stairs of the tall old house. I was probably passing through a phase of being fascinated by death, if unable to comprehend it, or else this appendage is a Freudian emblem of some sort. I knew that people who'd lived in the house were dead, I had a sense of generations and cemeteries, I went to primary school on the primary funeral route. We had a routine for pulling the blinds when a cortege passed, chanting the 'Our Father' together, moving on. So many things never leave you from this time of life: the smell of disinfectant in school corridors, the bulky radiators painted so many times thick spots had crusted into glands and scabs.

For a short time, I would have known my great-grandfather, William, as one of the old-world presences in the town – tweed suit, flat cap – before he went into the nursing home. I sense that, early on, I associated the man beneath the tree with him, or recognised the man beneath the tree as a type corresponding to William. I suppose one must remember how grotesque the very old can look to the very young; how generically uncanny.

After my great-grandfather had died, many years after in fact, my mother told me that he'd been a pioneer, a teetotaller, but not always. As a young man, drunk one night, he went astray on his way across the canal (it may even have been a mill pond then) and fell into the water. It was waist-deep, so he waded to the opposite end, abruptly, one presumes, sober. He washed up at home to recrimination and was, in the morning, deeply ashamed. He went straight to the church and took the pledge. When I heard this story of wading, repentance, shame, I wondered if my encounter at five was some kind of a time stutter, if I'd met his younger incarnation somehow, if during that experience of inebriation William himself had seen a weirdly daylit, flickering five-year-old regarding him from a cosmic height, if the chain of affect between us is nucleic.

There are issues with the timeline in this anecdote, of course. And, in all likelihood, the man under the tree was some town eccentric and not an apparition, problematically aged, from the past. It is all coincidence, and yet a great deal of poetic potential hinges on the sensation of self-consciousness at the centre of it.

It was this sensation, encased in the resinous effects of emotional deep time, that made it worthy of plucking and repurposing in a short story almost thirty years after the fact.

■

People say there are two things: guilt and shame. Guilt for what you have done, but shame at what you are.

In a book I came across as a student, the queer theorist Eve Kosofsky Sedgwick tries to explain shame itself – epiphenomenonally, as experience – by recalling herself walking in New York shortly after 9/11 and looking up to notice, jaggedly or disassociatively, that the twin towers were not there. Seeing, that is, or sensing the raw vacuum where death had happened and feeling, inexplicably, shame. I remember finding this account compelling because it is so weird: Sedgwick has done nothing to bring about the destruction of the twin towers and has nothing, rationally, to feel bad about. Nor is it the case of something so glib as feeling ashamed for humanity, ashamed of human nature, ashamed of one's complicity in foreign policy or any kind of political violence. Rather, the theorist feels *stupid*, naïve, or cowed for forgetting in this instant that the violence happened, for being taken by surprise at the harrowing absence in the sky. She feels, perhaps, mortal.

She also explains it – as I remember, or as I have decanted the details from a dense academic work I have no intention of tracking down again, for my own purposes – as a form of misidentification, of failed mirroring, whereby the person she thinks she is can be undone or dumbfounded simply by looking up and finding the environment that would otherwise facilitate this personhood vandalised.

This makes intuitive sense to me. With the man beneath the tree, when I was five, my shame and fright did not really occur in response to the narrative logic of the scenario – an old man passed out, coming to, under a tree – but to the fact that, just before this, I was in my own world, singing and running and separate from the group, a state I entered into all the time as a kid, because I was intensely sensitive and couldn't trust other people, especially groups of people, not to overwhelm me or absorb me or shout coarsely over me. In my own world I sustained a proud little privacy made of fantasises and ambient avenues – my own voice, my own footsteps, my own mental projections – in which I was left alone. And I must have understood the vain precarity of this enterprise to be so humiliated, so soundly *shamed*, at its interruption by someone I feel, in the thick space of this enduring and textured memory, occultly responsible for.

▪

When I began writing my first novel I was bored, and I don't mean idly – I mean violently. Giving vent to this violent boredom helped. At the start I imagined I might have a coy kind of epigraph opening everything breathily: *'I am half-sick of shadows,' said / The Lady of Shalott*. This lady leaves boredom and the consolations of simulacrum to choose life (Lancelot) and, ultimately, death. On a basic level she would rather be dead than left behind to imagine the parties going on elsewhere. In the painting of the same name by John William Waterhouse, the lady lifts her arms in a pose of frustration and stretches her back, her face angled wryly upwards as she side-eyes her own reflection. I liked the epigraph idea because it was slightly over the top and I intended the novel, the enterprise itself, to be slightly over the top.

Which is partly why the original title was *How They Met Themselves* – in some lurking nether-reaches of American Amazon, it is still purchasable as *How They Met Themselves* – after the Dante Gabriel Rossetti painting from 1864. In this painting a honeymoon couple, the artist and his wife, Elizabeth Siddal, wear mediaeval clothes like good Pre-Raphaelites and meet their own doppelgängers walking in a gloomy forest. Siddal faints away with arms extended in a pose loosely suggestive of Victorian melodrama, perhaps because meeting one's double is a sign of impending death, and the work itself was finished in the aftermath of the real Siddal's death by laudanum overdose in 1862. Siddal's own illustration of the Lady of Shalott, a pencil sketch, shows a plainer, thinner lady glancing preoccupied from her loom as if distracted rather wearily by, say, an unwanted knock; before the window to Camelot is a crucifix.

My first encounter with the Tennyson poem was indirect, through the Pixies' 'Nimrod's Son' and, specifically, its riff on the curse of the cracked mirror: *the joke is come upon me*. But even without this watermark emerging through later encounters in adulthood the inference is pretty punk. I've always been drawn to doubles. Or, rather, to the idea of self as a representative template, an automaton, which is detached from the lived experience of being alive – in the novel (which wound up being titled *This Happy*) this concern began life as an interest in parallel lives or possible lives and junctions in life which mark the difference between one kind of life and another, but also of being badly seen, misunderstood, perhaps even instrumentalised by another person because they think you are kind of *are*, in a way, an automaton: a symbol, a thing.

As a young woman I experienced this from men who took certain details about my life – my writing, for instance, or my bookishness or my physical smallness or my youth or the ersatz bohemianism with which I appeared to live vis-à-vis the nine-to-five life – and extrapolated from these with speed to decide I represented something – freedom, creative energy, self-possession – they themselves, in fact, desired. Because I was young I could not see this abrupt and flattering response to my sitting there or standing there or whatever as illusory and, for the man concerned, simulacral: I can say kindly now they saw something in me as effigy and responded to it with psychodrama. Certainly women behave the same way and I don't mean to suggest this is only misogynist (though it can have that flavour, at times). However, it *is* terribly painful to be made feel you have failed for being human by a person who decided, on sight, that you were a symbol instead. This person will also find it easier to leave or to be cruel because they are talking to a doll.

I began the novel in the aftermath of a brief and bruising relationship that was not a relationship but two people awkwardly interacting in a strange sentimental submarine, one very young and one far too old, and this distance unmendable, incomprehensible, like little kids who can't speak yet handing one another toys as tokens of tensely hopeful affection. It was not his fault but afterwards I looked at the drab matter of my life, then nine-to-five, and decided that madness in my submarine, death-drive, was preferable to weaving simulacra, sitting outside life with my hands dabbing listlessly at a shining machine, and these are – always have been – the same bonily elongated and uncanny hands that made my precursors so successful at topping and manually finishing hose that even I heard about this, like, one hundred years afterwards.

My sister's iterations are better: hands like hands of a tanned skeleton, which she keeps in high style with shellac.

If you're a complicated woman you have to go mad once, and preferably only once, after which you see everything clearly. To recover, and right before I took to the book, I decided to learn to meditate by signing up for a donation-based ten-day residential course in Vipassanā (no talking, no gadgets, no writing, no reading, no input from the world), hosted by kindly vegan votives in an off-season boarding school. Rule one of Vipassanā instruction is that, for the duration, one cannot kill a living thing, and this extends to the moths and bluebottles wilting or zipping through a dormitory I remember now as gauzy behind drawn curtains and smelling gently of medicine.

Because there is an entire (respectful, informative) genre of writing about white people discovering Vipassanā, I will not rhapsodise: suffice to say I was in an agony of imagined inflammation during each two-hour stint of entirely inert meditation, but this pain evaporated as soon as I stood up; suffice to say a pollarded monkey-puzzle tree of muttering rooks seemed to address me personally each day as I sat on a window ledge imbibing the only stimulant I could get hold of, which was fucking Barleycup; suffice to say for three days I could not get Josh Ritter album filler out of my head until suddenly, unbidden, 'Salisbury Hill' replaced it summarily, just like that, as I washed my hands in the communal bathroom. A lot of the paperwork ahead of entry seemed to suggest certain people were predisposed to psychotic break when undergoing the silence and focus and loneliness required for Vipassanā, but everyone there seemed placidly elegant, ducking between buildings with insular gazes and walking slowly, at break times, around a playing field lined with green ditches and hawthorn trees.

And at the end, on the final day, we broke our silence and our semi-fast to talk to one another animatedly at last. The warmth between twenty women who've been sleeping side by side and holding doors open for one another for two weeks without meeting eyes, without speaking – twenty women watching one another's gestures and gaits and habits and haircuts in silent calculation – was remarkable. We told one another about our assumptions. We said, I think you do X for a living and come from X and I think you have children/do not have children; I think you teach X or like X and you remind of me Y.

More than one told me something about myself, my life, which is not true but which I have always, always wanted to be true. They said to me: I bet you are a dancer, aren't you? I'm not and I have never been able to dance. Tap and jazz was a one-year thing; after that, it was being asked to stand at the back of the room during ceili and a photograph, from 1997, showing me skinnily screwed up, fist-clenched, midway through a choreographed Spice Girls routine. The photograph is testament to my profound self-consciousness and shyness as a child; it hurts me to look at it, since I look miserable at nine. To have seen a dancer as I moved about for ten days, brushing my teeth and folding my mat and lurking with Barleycup under some rooks, was to see some longing aspiration made incarnate in a set of gestures, affectations, disconnected from reality.

I think of this on those mornings when you wake at dawn and for a minute, less than that, feel painfully baffled by your own first name, your age, your own vertiginous history – those glittering interims of possibility and panic when every single thing about you seems so shamefully arbitrary.

■

At Halloween: Finglas is ablaze. You can see it from the train, like Mount Olympus, like Slievenamon on fire in the fairy tale. I sit in the wrecked kitchen of a houseshare that has, really, been going on too long – extended into the late thirties of the men involved, all of whom are musicians, none of whom mind the weird pergola rotting under plant debris in the back garden nor the smell of mildew nor the darkness of the hall, where there is no bulb anymore. The housemates tell me their visiting friend has an alcohol problem and will certainly encourage everyone to continue partying into the next day. Actually, we sing 'Wuthering Heights' and then begin telling ghost stories.

Here is one: a teenage girl sleeping by the disused chimney breast of a Victorian house in Dublin 3 is woken repeatedly by solid, persistent, deliberate human knocking from within the coffined confine of the chimney breast.

Here is one: bandmates on a tour in Eastern Europe descend the stairs of an industrial building after midnight on their way backstage and meet a middle-aged man, bushy-moustached, in mid-century military regalia; whipped by fright, they turn in unison and belt back up the stairs without discussing it.

Here is one: a group of youth hostelers meet the wandering spirit of the country-and-western icon John Denver walking around the bend of a boreen; he retreats from them, clasping prayer hands and bowing, without turning around to look at Eurydice. On his back is a guitar case.

Here is one: I saw, I say, *quite possibly* the spirit of my great-grandfather pressed through time and deeply confused, young and old at once, spreading over my vision like a stain.

And this, you see, is how stories get made.

Conception

BRENDA ROMERO

Welcome to *Conception*! *Conception* is a one- to two-player game in which a player tries to make a baby with the aid of science. Hoping for successful egg retrieval, the player tries for zygotes, blastocysts, implantation and, if all goes well in nine months, you have a baby or two.

What's in the box?

Conception has the following components:

- one ovary;
- ten egg follicles (grey tokens);
- ten matured eggs (white tokens);
- one right fallopian tube, ruined due to an ectopic pregnancy at twenty-one;
- one left fallopian tube, ruined due to another ectopic pregnancy at twenty-seven (they took the ovary with it);
- one retroverted uterus (abnormal);
- one penis (optional);

- two-hundred to five-hundred million sperm (overkill, really, but average);
- one four-sided die;
- one six-sided die; and
- an indeterminate amount of money, but at least $1,000 (please supply your own).

Set-up

Place the game bits in front of you on a table, like so:

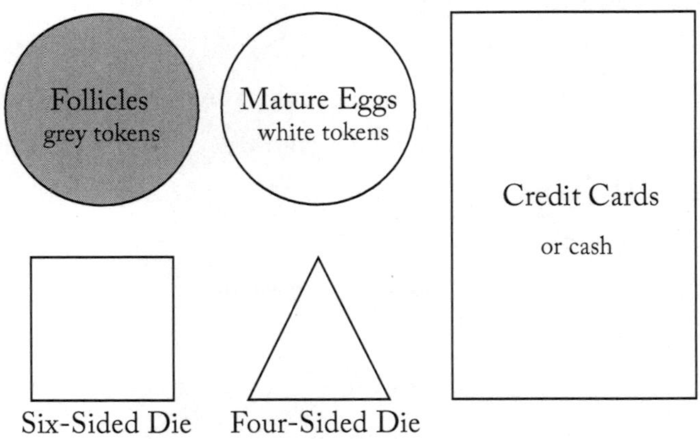

Starting the game

Take the four-sided die and roll it. Look below.

1. You live in Canada, so the procedure is free because you

have a full tubal blockage. While you never considered this a bonus, your tubes' absolutely shambolic state moves you to the front of the infertility line and qualifies you for free treatment. You need $6,000 for the medication. You cannot start the game unless you have the money.

2. You live in Massachusetts, so the procedure is free because the state legislature mandates that all insurance companies that cover birth must also cover infertility treatment for women who need it. This also covers part of your medication. You need $1,000 to pay for the rest. You cannot start the game unless you have the money.
3. You live in California, so the procedure is expensive. This is a wealthy state and wealthy people live here. Don't like it, move; and sometimes you think about it because you come from a poor family and you don't feel like you belong here. You need $13,000 for the procedure and $6,000 for medication. Your business is doing well, though, so this is achievable. A family member comes into your life unexpectedly and needs to live with you, and so you put it off. This is the end of your game.
4. You live in Ireland, so the procedure is on sale compared to California. You can afford it. You get the blood work done and make an appointment with the fertility clinic. He tells you that you're too old and while he could do it, sure, there's no chance. Nothing would take. Nothing would fertilize. If it did, it wouldn't be viable. He smiles at you and says that he won't charge you for the visit, as if

that was even on your mind. You want to reroll, but the four-sided die is missing. You suspect he took it in lieu of payment. You're not surprised. Maybe you left it there. This is the end of your game.

If you have the money, you can play the game.

Playing the game

She who cares the most goes first. Technically, the second player doesn't need to be here and, often, he's not. *Conception* is broken down into six quests, each of which is displayed on the game board:

1. Needles and ovaries
2. Get the eggs
3. Fertilization
4. Implantation
5. Pregnancy
6. Birth

Needles and ovaries

Most women mature one egg per month, but not you. You have one ovary left, so you probably mature one egg every other month. The doctors give you medication, which overstimulates your lone ovary. Hopefully, you will get a lot of follicles.

Take the six-sided die and roll it. Then look below.

1. It's late 1999 and you're in Ottawa, Canada. You are sitting on the bus and can't remember whether you just got on and are *going* to work or have been on the bus and are coming *back* from work. You realize this is not OK and you call your doctor. Apparently, you're having a reaction to the fertility drugs and you're ordered to stop them immediately. You're crushed. 'What about the eggs,' you say? 'We'll have to try again in a month,' they tell you. Go back to the start. Fortunately, you can take ninety per cent of your drug money with you. You start to feel like it's 'drug money' in the seedy sense, too, because you're not earning a lot and it takes twenty per cent of your gross income to get these drugs. You can cross out this option now. At least they know that these meds don't work for you and they'll give you something different next time.
2. It's early January in 2000 and you're in Ottawa, Canada. You are on a new course of meds and can now at least remember whether you're coming or going. At your appointment, you discover that you have five follicles. You've read stories of women getting ten, twelve, fourteen eggs and you feel a bit let down and lonely for your missing ovary. You're sure it would have done better, or at least cheered on your good ovary if it were still present. Still, five follicles are better than none. You continue taking fertility drugs and move to the next step. Take five grey follicle tokens.

3. You try not to look at pregnant women, but you do. You marvel that this just works for other people. Sometimes, when you're feeling off, you think of a woman who lived in the same trailer park as you. She found out she was pregnant and celebrated by getting drunk. 'That's not good for the baby,' you told her. 'I'm only having two,' she said. You doubted it. Roll again.
4. It's late April in 2000 and you're still in Ottawa, Canada. You're on the same meds but back again because you rolled poorly in the next step of the game, so things didn't work out (you'll see when you get there). This time, though, they up the dosage because they have your last round as an indicator. You have nine follicles. You're delighted. *Good on ya, ovary*. For once, you don't think about your other, missing ovary. Take nine grey follicle tokens.
5. It's late 2003 and you're in Springfield, Massachusetts. You bring your file with you from the last ovarian stimulation in Ottawa and they put you on the same cocktail of fertility drugs. This time, you get three follicles. You're disappointed. The nurse says 'it only takes one' and you try to be cheerful about this. You figure out the exact odds of success in your head before the smile even fades from her face. Take three grey follicle tokens.
6. You are told to give yourself the injections in your butt. You decide to do it in the leg instead. It hurts less and the doctor tells you it's OK. The drugs are all you think about:

how much they are worth; how important it is to take them on time; and how many follicles they might be making. You start to think, *if it doesn't work this time, I'll do it again*. You don't know where you'll get the money. Roll again.

You're ready for your egg retrieval. Move on to the next step.

Get the eggs

An appointment is made for your egg retrieval. Thirty-six hours before and not a minute late, you inject the drug that's designed to mature the eggs in their little follicles. You can see them on the ultrasound, like little black spots on a snowball.

Take the six-sided die and roll it. Then look below.

1. You're in Ottawa, Canada. You've never been through this before. You arrive for your retrieval and they take you into the operating theatre. You think they'll put you under for the process, but the nurse tells you that's not the case. 'You're awake through the whole thing', she says. 'Then how do they get them?' you ask. 'You should tell squeamish people to stop reading now,' she replies. They wheel you into the operating theatre and prep you like you're in for an exam with your gynecologist. 'We'll insert an ultrasound probe into your vagina and then use a needle that's connected to a vacuum of sorts.' You pause.

The mental map of your anatomy does not include a secret direct passage from vagina to ovary. 'Where's that needle going? Through my vagina?' They tell you it won't hurt much and it doesn't at first, just a brief internal pain as it passes through. The aspiration of the eggs, however, is *Dark Souls*-level pain and you cry out with each effort. 'Don't move at all,' they say, 'it will be over soon.' Trade your grey follicle tokens for mature egg tokens.

2. You've never been so acutely aware of an internal body part. You think of your ovary constantly, fearful that the eggs will escape before the doctor comes to collect them. Roll again.
3. You're in Ottawa, Canada. This is your second time through the aspiration process. You already know that they will pierce your vaginal wall with a needle. It's not that you're worried about – it's the extreme pain from the aspiration. You wonder if that's what it feels like to be kicked in the nuts. 'Don't move,' they tell you. You try to focus on the ultrasound screen, watching the little black pools on the snowball disappear one by one. Trade your grey follicle tokens for mature egg tokens.
4. You sit in clinic waiting rooms with other women, all on the same desperate quest, each asking one or both of the following questions: 'How many times can I do this before I run out of money?' and 'How many times can I do this before my body gives out?' You commit to doing it as many times as it takes. You have no idea where the

money will come from, but reason that some of these women don't either, and they just keep going. The feeling of desperation comes regularly to you, your life now filled with needles and injections. Your mornings are rituals of pulling sterilized water from its vial, injecting it into the drugs, swirling drug dust and water around before drawing it back into the needle. You forage with the needle for every bit of wetness against the glass vial walls, leaving none back. Every little bit matters. Every little bit could be the difference between one and none. Roll again.

5. You're in Springfield, Massachusetts. This is your third go at egg retrieval. In the operating theatre, the nurse approaches you to connect you to an IV. 'What's that for?' you ask. 'To administer drugs,' she says. 'To put me under?' 'Of course,' she tells you, 'you can't do this awake.' You tell her that you have, twice. She seems surprised to hear this and asks where. 'Ottawa,' you say. She smiles and empties a syringe into the IV's catheter. A warm rush floods into your arm. 'You should start to feel relaxed soon,' she says. Trade your grey follicle tokens for mature egg tokens.
6. You dream that you are pregnant. You think of the follicles as proto-babies and you grow attached to them. Roll again.

Leave your mature egg follicles with the clinic. Move on to the next step.

Fertilization

While the clinic waits for the eggs, the sperm goes through an actual wash-and-spin cycle. Only the best sperm are selected. It seems like a fitting domestic task, this washing and spinning, in preparation for an arranged marriage of egg and sperm. You think of how this happens, with sweaty, drunken abandon, in the back seats of cars, in fields, in beds and on couches.

Wait four days. Take the six-sided die and roll it. Then look below.

1. You're in Ottawa, Canada. You've spent four days excitedly thinking about whether the doctor will put in all your fertilized eggs or freeze some. The phone rings. 'None of your eggs fertilized,' the doctor says. 'But I had enough eggs,' you say. 'I'm sorry,' he replies. You can cross out this option now. Pathology figures out what the problem is. 'Hard-shelled eggs,' they say. 'You're kidding me,' I say. They're not. There's another term for it, but this is the term you remember. Go back to the start. You will have to pay again should you play again.
2. A friend calls to tell you that she's pregnant. She can't believe it. From your hollowness you say, 'Congratulations, I'm so happy for you', and you want to be, but you feel nothing. Roll again.
3. You're in Ottawa, Canada. You've been through this once before. This time, they know that you have hard-shelled eggs and so they take no chances. Using a microscope, they select a perfect sperm and inject it into your egg. You

marvel that someone thought of this and that there are needles so small. If you dropped one, would you ever find it? After four days, the phone rings. 'One egg fertilized,' they say. 'That's good,' you say, but you knew there were more. 'It only takes one,' they tell you. You do the math in your head and wish you weren't so good at math. Take one mature egg token and leave the rest.

4. You're in Springfield, Massachusetts. You think of the clinic's waiting room as you wait for them to call – chairs around a centre table, the anxious, hopeful excitement of infertile women as they glance at one another, sizing each other up, calculating odds based on online charts they've committed to memory. The doctor calls to tell you the good news.
    i. If you have only one mature egg, you say, 'It's better than none. It's you and me, egg.' Take one mature egg token and go to the next step.
    ii. If you have multiple matured eggs, you say, 'That's great!' Take three mature egg tokens and go to the next step.
5. You imagine a woman in the 1940s, sitting by the fire and staring into her tea. She wants a child, but her womb is barren. You wonder if she thinks about the future, wishing she could be you, a woman who at least has a chance. Roll again.
6. A woman you mentor becomes pregnant from a one-night stand and decides to terminate the pregnancy. It's

incredibly difficult for her and she comes to you bereft. You support her, console her and hold her while she cries. 'You made the right choice for you,' you say. You cry. Roll again.

Leave your fertilized eggs with the clinic. Move on to the next step.

Implantation

The clinic tells you to come back in four days, once the fertilized eggs have reached the blastocyst stage. It's peculiar to think of your proto-babies growing in a lab. You arrive for your appointment, dress in a sterile gown and walk into the operating theatre. 'Hop up here,' they say. Placing the ultrasound on your belly, your uterus appears on the screen. They guide a medical-grade straw into place and force its contents out. The ultrasound tech gives you a picture of this moment. The straw looks like a snow-covered road at night, winding through your womb. Hopefully, they stick.

You can lie down for a while at home if you want. Move on to the next step.

Pregnancy

Now you wait. It's the first thing you think about when you wake. You wish your body had a window so that you could peek in to see what's happening. It's the end of the road or the beginning of another. You wish for a pay-to-rush mechanic like they have in games, where you hand over cash to cut the time in half.

Wait twenty days. Take the six-sided die and roll. Look below.

1. You can't wait the twenty days and get a pregnancy test at the store. It's negative, but it's only been ten days. What did you expect? Roll again.
2. You wait seventeen days and travel from Ottawa, Canada, to visit your mother in New York. You bleed into the toilet and shout 'I'm losing the baby!', although it's probably just your period. Appearing at the bathroom door, your mother asks, 'What's wrong?' 'I've lost the baby!' you cry. Panicked, hopped up on fertility drugs, you reach for the phone to call your then-husband, who is away on business and staying with his mother. 'He's not home,' she says. You call again. She tells you again, again and again that he's not home at 11 p.m., 1 a.m., 3 a.m. and 5 a.m. Finally, he is there at 8 a.m. 'Where were you?' you ask. You're in tears. Before you can say what's happened to you, he tells you some lies and tries to get his mother to corroborate. He hands her the phone to do so, but she blows up on you instead. You say nothing as she yells and calls you names, maybe out of exhaustion or the horrible situation her son has put her in. Broken down, you listen for five minutes, waiting for her anger to pass, but it doesn't. You hand the phone to your own mother, who tries to calm her, repeating her name again

and again, 'Margaret, Margaret, Margaret.' Eventually, your mother places the handset on the receiver, hanging up even as Margaret continues, something you've never seen your mother do before. 'Come here,' she says. Later that day he calls, and you tell him what happened. Go back to the start. You will have to pay again should you play again.

3. Games are ultimately about wish fulfilment. You wish for this to end well. Twenty days is a very long time. Roll again.
4. You can't wait the twenty days and get a pregnancy test at the store. It's negative, but it's only been fifteen days. What did you expect? You throw it in the garbage and wash off the pee from your hands. Looking down you see a faint, blue line forming. 'Holy fuck,' you say aloud. 'I'm pregnant.' Move immediately to the next step.
5. The clinic schedules an appointment for a pregnancy test on the twentieth day after implantation. On day eleven, you go to the pharmacy and purchase four pregnancy tests, including two with early detection. You wonder what the clerk must think. You pee on the stick, but mostly on your hand because you want to make sure you hit it. There is a plus sign in the little window. 'My god,' you say. 'I'm pregnant.' Move immediately to the next step.
6. You explain to friends how quickly the attachment forms. 'From the moment they put that egg inside of me, I believed myself pregnant.' Not an intellectual belief, but something different and deeper, something instinctual.

You think of how many eggs fertilize, fail to implant and pass right on through, the proto-mother none the wiser. But from the moment the egg enters you, attachment grows whether it seeds or not.

Endgame

You love the thought of babies moving inside of you, even if you can't feel them. Even the thought that there is a baby in there pleases you. You've come a long way.

Take the six-sided die and roll it. Then look below. (Or maybe don't look this time and just have it end the way you want it to end, the way you wish it could end for everyone who plays *Conception*.)

1. You give birth to a baby girl, whose legs are so strong that she stands up the day she is born. 'I've been waiting for you,' you say to her. She grows to be a fine young woman, intelligent and driven – someone you'd want to be your friend. You think back to the times with her still inside you, sitting at the bus stop, talking to her and waiting for her to move.
2. You pull down your pants to pee and see blood on your underwear. It can't be. You were pregnant. You saved the test results and you can prove it. You wipe yourself to see if it's coming from there, and it is. You wait and wipe again, just in case. You sit on the toilet until the hard plastic seat becomes uncomfortable. Tears fall onto your bare legs.

3. You give birth to twins, a boy and a girl so different from one another you joke that they could be born of different donors, but they were not. You hear their baby laughs and remember how they moved their little legs when they were excited. One wants to be a doctor and the other a lawyer. You love to watch their minds work.
4. Nine months is such a long time. You worry about delivering early and research premature babies. Every move, every kick, every weird feeling concerns you. You map out six months, maybe seven. When both pass, you exhale. Roll again.
5. You lose the pregnancy. Sobbing, you confide in several friends, some of whom tell you that 'it was for the best' and 'thankfully, you weren't too far along'. Hollowness follows barrenness, apparently. You know they mean well, but the words break what little of you is left. *It was not for the best*, you think. *It doesn't matter how far along I was.* You visit this potential person often, marking their imaginary milestones in your mind.
6. You give birth to a baby boy. He is early and not ready for the world. You visit him daily in the NICU and watch him grow, fight and survive. You bring him home, swaddled in a newborn blanket that feels the size of a tarp on his little limbs. He pees on you while you change his diaper. Surprised, you say, 'Oh no!' Hearing your voice, he giggles, and you hear his beautiful little laugh – his perfect little laugh – for the very first time.

An interview with Claire-Louise Bennett

JENNIFER HODGSON

In *Checkout 19* the life of the mind belongs to a girl and often she takes long, long baths in the afternoon, her big, fuck-off brain floating on a scented cloud of Body Shop banana shampoo and Rothmans. Claire-Louise Bennett's new book is the story of a life lived among and through and sometimes in spite of books. It departs, however, from those old metaphysics, which now feel stretched thinner than ever, about the capacity of culture to redeem our experience or enable us to levitate out of our material circumstances. 'As if the only thing you could do with a book was read it', says the narrator at one point. *As if!* Bennett is interested in the experiential nuances of being transformed and transported by taking in and being taken in by language and writing. Here people seem to want to let themselves to fall to pieces far more than they want to gather themselves together and become a character.

Checkout 19 is a kind of bildungsroman, sure, but one in which (as in the work of Annie Ernaux, or Tillie Olsen, or Carolyn Steedman – and not nearly enough others, we're crying out for more like this) Bennett chronicles the attempt at *making* for oneself, by necessity, rather than simply managing to *find*, a place in language and in the world. There's a line from the end of Olsen's 'I Stand Here Ironing' that has caught painfully in me ever since I first read it. It's when the narrator wonders what will become of her strange and wilful and inward young daughter, raised with not enough money and no end of strife: 'Let her be. So all that is in her will not bloom – but in how many does it? There is still enough left to live by.' *Enough left to live by*. I like to think that *Checkout 19* is responding: but what if she did bloom? What would she do, what would she have to say, with all that is in her?

Jennifer Hodgson (JH): From its epigraph, taken from Ingeborg Bachmann's *Malina*, onwards, *Checkout 19* considers what it is that we're about when we're reading and writing. But your account is different to the ones we often hear, that lean on shibboleths like moral value, or self-knowledge, or existential consolation. Can you tell us about the experiences of reading and writing you're exploring in the book?

Claire-Louise Bennett (CLB): The experiences of reading and writing in *Checkout 19* are based upon the role and impact both have had, and continue to have, on my life – my life as it is conceived, and how it is lived, day to day. Some time ago I read a psychologist saying that we are born into fantasy and only gradually acquire a sense of 'reality'. That seems about right to me. Fantasy feels like the source and basis of my being, it feels like the most real and instructive aspect of my psyche – if I want to understand a situation better, if I need some insight into why I am behaving and feeling as I do, it is to this realm that I turn and delve into. Books are on the threshold, aren't they? There's a thrilling blurring of fantasy and reality that goes on when one reads and writes. Put simply, something imagined, or read, can exist so strongly, almost violently, within one, on and on, and these forces and presences exert considerable influence on what and who we are drawn to and repelled by in the exterior world – many of the decisions we make in the out-and-about world have their basis in this imaginary zone. There's nothing irrational about that – if it seems irrational it's only that it's a dimension of existence and becoming that goes largely unexamined. Reality is an illusion, that's just how it's always seemed to me – like a game really – which meant that there were certain things, things that should incentivise a person to cultivate ordained goals and so on, that I couldn't take seriously at all, they had no meaning to me. That perspective can leave a person drifting around in a very remote place with no impetus. But I'm not a nihilist. Books and writing enable me to negotiate and relish the illusory aspect of reality, and to identify the truths and signals in fantasy.

Checkout 19 is frequently described as 'a book about books'; really it's about language. The intertextuality throughout makes the literary aspect of the narrator's love and exploration of language very apparent, but the spoken word is absolutely crucial to her also. Growing up I never saw my father read a single book, but his use of language was riotous, so inventive and playful, in an almost Joycean way – well I think of him as being 'piratey', he loves words like 'carbuncle' and 'goiter' and 'gizzards' and 'wingnut' and 'charminations' – he and my mum made up quite a lot of words actually, like 'googybarger', which refers to gonads. Ha! Very fun. Natalia Ginzburg's book *Family Lexicon* really captures the power of these sayings and oddities that every family has. *Checkout 19* is full of them, as much as it is full of books, because despite not being literary people my family and their rascally way with words have contributed to and continue to fuel my passion for language.

JH: *Checkout 19* makes clear that not everyone is permitted a life in letters, or a life where it is possible to think and express freely and fearlessly. You write of a young person's 'thumping' sense of expectancy and optimism, and how that life force gets cut down by the injunction to 'get real' and 'face up to reality'. You've spoken elsewhere about the impediments – financial, practical, social, cultural, psychological – that being from a working-class background presents for writers, as well as the richness of modes of expression that are rooted in working-class experience: the phenomenological strangeness of being inducted into a world not made for you, the perceptual effects of living hand-to-mouth, of shared houses and thin walls. You've also mentioned your own (recent?) reconciliation with what you call your 'long-lost working-class self'. Did this prompt the writing of the book?

CLB: I've lived in Ireland for many years, most of my life in fact, and for many years whenever I was asked what had brought me here I'd say something facetious, such as 'a cheap Ryanair flight', that kind of thing. I avoided answering or even addressing the question. The fact is I left England in order to escape living a life that would have been utterly at odds with who I am, what I value, and what I need to do in order to feel at ease in the world. The options available to me there were very narrow, and that has a lot to do with the class I was born into, and being a woman of course. So I was reflecting upon these factors – writing, womanhood, class – that have contributed to the shape of my life and during this period I discovered the work of Annie Ernaux, and Tove Ditlevsen, and the way these women write about promise, of discovering their intellectual and creative power, of having to conceal it, of having to pretend to be less smart than they are, of how terrifying the prospect of adulthood is because you don't know how you are going to support yourself, and so on, all of that resonated with me, it floored me really. I'd never really thought about it very much, you just get on with things don't you, because there's always some bugger that's worse off, so why would you make a big deal of whatever challenge you're facing from one day to the next? And then more recently again I noticed some articles cropping up in the British newspapers about university students there being picked on because of the way they spoke – they had regional accents – and that made me livid. Some of the people doing the bullying were teachers. Imagine that. I felt sickened and bloodthirsty. Nothing has changed since I left, if anything there are strong grounds for supposing they have got worse.

Ann Quin is another writer I've only relatively recently discovered and who also impacted upon how *Checkout 19* became what it is. Reading her work brought to my attention the phenomenologically oriented mode of expression that coming from a working-class background encourages. More so, in my own work certainly, than a psychological turn. And maybe that's because intrinsic to the phenomenological mode is a bid for freedom. As I understand it, the aim of describing the quotidian well is to write according to one's own direct experience as closely and as faithfully as possible, without deferring to received ideas and conventional formulations, and in this way one develops a rigorous yet malleable personal epistemology – one is therefore free. To describe well you must suspend orthodox values and ascribed meanings, ditch them entirely, so there is a loosening of categories, the inanimate, for example, is made vital and the animate deadly or borrowed or counterfeit, or whatever, everything is in flux, and of course you want that if you're from the lower end of society, of course you want to shake it all loose, because why on earth do you want to perpetuate the notion that things are set in stone if you've got the shorter end of the stick?

JH: There's an idea of narrative running through the book that's far broader than the literary. You seem to be considering the emplotment of peoples' lives – and what happens if you refuse the story that's been written on your behalf. And also: how one can reconcile the human tendency to make sense of our experience by fictionalising it with a capacity for presence, with thinking about and feeling things as they are. Your work seems to propose a departure from narrative, towards sentences, intensities, atmospheres, moods, tones. How far does this awareness of narrative's power to shape a life and a self, and the resistance to that pull, inform your writing?

CLB: The awareness of the power of narrative is something I felt most acutely in relation to my life and how I might live it, and the realisation that, as you put it, the road ahead of me was a story already written on my behalf, and that living meant simply going along with this story, this off-the-peg one-size-fits all construct. But it didn't fit, or I didn't fit, and there were a number of years where this not-fitting caused me a lot of confusion and distress, not least because I couldn't see what alternatives there were – society seems quite intent on endorsing and reinforcing a very limited idea of what a life can be, based entirely around economic imperatives which are, at this stage, totally unsustainable. But governments won't deviate from models of so-called growth, it's sickening – growth and consumption, growth and consumption – we've used everything up, there is nothing left to consume, and we are producing so much waste there's nowhere left for it to go. And then of course you're made to feel like a misfit or a failure if you don't go along with all that and deem material wealth to be the marker of a life well lived. So naturally my attitude to this has always impacted on how I go about representing life and direct experience on the page. My writing is not 'fragmented' or 'non-linear' or whatever for the sake of it, just to be clever or different – not at all – as much as it's a stylistic trait it is also a political matter, an ethical matter. Creating a cogent narrative is the aim of analysis I believe, and a tale well told does have its consolations, but I don't write to console myself or other people, and I don't enjoy writing that is permeated with that intention, in fact I find those sorts of books inexorably alienating. I don't read to be consoled. I read to hurt well, to hurt better – I am perennially drawn to books that enable me to experience pain in slow motion, and in that way I am perhaps gradually acquiring an exquisitely calibrated sense of my own suffering, and how and why other human beings suffer on and on.

JH: *Checkout 19* moves between the first-person singular, third-person singular and first-person plural – between 'I' and 'she' and 'we'. The self here feels non-continuous and multiple. What made you decide to render perspective like this?

CLB: 'She' is one of my favourite words. It's almost mythical. When I think 'she' I immediately see the figures of many women in various states of motion, carved into a grainy light blonde stone. Sometimes 'she' has wings. Sometimes 'she' is digging. Sometimes 'she' is reaching. Sometimes 'she' is behind me in the supermarket, and I am the 'she' in front of her. When I was young, the way people, women especially, said 'she' was very different from how they said 'he'. It was often said with a tantalising emphasis that arose from a bizarre conflation of disapproval and admiration, of propriety and salaciousness. It was as if the fact that there was a 'she' at all was both a miracle and an affront, simultaneously. Sometimes I am that 'she' to whom these conflicted attitudes of wonder and disapprobation are directed, and I enjoy that, it makes me feel torn and timeless. And 'we' – well, for many years I felt like a Russian doll, with lots of mes tucked into one another, of which of course only one, the outer shell, is visible to the external world. I liked to commune and conspire with the smallest one, deep within, complete and seamless as a skittle, but absolutely impossible to topple or sway.

JH: In the originary scene of writing in the book, writing springs forth out of drawing or, actually, doodling. Suddenly, quite without meaning to, the narrator finds herself not doodling anymore but writing. I'm curious as to whether this link between two kinds of 'mark-making', and the idea that writing extends from drawing rather than from speaking, from the voice, apply to your own writing?

CLB: Springs from a failure to draw! A frustration – drawing is a limited mode of expression for her – she's hopeless at it, she can't depict anything realistically, and the doodles are as insubstantial and recursive as those transparent creatures that skim and shudder at the very edges of our vision and scarper the moment we try to hold them in our gaze. The phrase 'mark-making' gives me an atavistic shudder – doesn't it refer to a primordial urge to leave one's trace? Of asserting 'I was here'. Whereas speech is concerned with conveying 'I am here'. I feel my own writing is driven by both of these functions, and very probably by a third: 'I will not always be here'.

JH: In the book, there's a tension between secrecy and exposure. On the one hand, the narrator savours her inner, imaginative world, against the risk of sharing it with others: of getting into trouble, of not being understood and, moreover, of there being no place in the world to put what's within her. On the other, she longs to be connected with everything else, to be more than herself. Expression feels like a fraught but very heady, sometimes transgressive, thing. Writing and reading are closely affiliated with desiring, with wanting to be inside another person, or being where you're not meant to be, or unmasking yourself and others. All this reminded me of a passage towards the end of *Pond*, where the narrator tells themselves: 'Sooner or later you're going to have to speak up.' Is this book in part preoccupied by finding a way to reconcile the two sides of this conflict?

CLB: What does Bachmann say in *Malina*? 'Expression is insanity, it arises out of our insanity.' I'm not concerned with reconciling conflict, not between secrecy and exposure, nor between my intellectual life and my very ordinary beginnings, which still constitute a considerable part of my personality, and will always do so. An element of Ernaux's work that is so poignant for me is that this fundamental schism is never resolved, her sense of shame that arises from feeling she is a class defector endures – a seamless transition from one social strata to the other because of her success is not achieved. I am criss-crossed with contradictions, my work is criss-crossed with contradictions – and so too is much of the work of my favourite authors. Consistent people give me the creeps. Whoever really trusts the smooth!

JH: One of the things I like most about reading your writing is the completely virtuosic list-making. I wonder where that came from, and about the pleasures of it in your own writing process?

CLB: List-making has always been a natural feature of my writing. Inventories reveal what and how I see, and I like where they take me. They almost always begin in the physical world, with what is in front of me, and these mundane items trigger associations, they connect with and conjure up phenomena that isn't in front of me but is always present in me – so a list charts reality and fantasy bouncing off one another. What entity is provoked in my imagination by a material object I see – and what do the things I imagine encourage me to notice in the physical world? I feel as if I am expanding and contracting the world around me when I'm making these lists. Added to which, I think it's liberating for a word not to always be caught up in a sentence, negated by contributing to the conveyance of a broader meaning that it is totally unaware of, while it sits there, credulously, fourth or fifth in a row, like a witless innocent in a line-up.

JH: *Checkout 19*, like *Pond*, is a book preoccupied with darkness and shadows, with the idea that underneath what's visible there's a core of undifferentiated, 'squirming' darkness. Both books seem to propose sitting among these shadows, rather than banishing them, as what you call 'companions, really, yes, and not as sad as all that'. Are writing and reading a means of welcoming them in?

CLB: The unknowable, the inexplicable, the indeterminate, the unfamiliar, the disquieting, the baffling, the fake, the passion, the unwashed, the forbidden, the lost, the delirious, the repressed, the unexplained, the wasted, the inconsolable, the abyss, the dread, the unnamed, the impossible, the ominous, the unformed, the shamed, the chasm, the talisman, the outcast, the flicker, the infatuation, the doubt, the yearning, the unbearable, the brink, the gasp, the unexpected, the ineffable, the irresolute, the schism, the nemesis, the obscure, the rejected, the congenital, the reversal, the she-wolf, the hurtful, the exception, the invisible, the changeling, the dwindling, the trespasser, the hidden, the uncontrollable, the promise, the dare, the bastard, the unwanted, the unsaid, the unsound, the dream, the aside, the faraway, the bogus, the reoccurring, the lump, the delusion, the secret, the curse, the deception, the arousing, the deviation, the unavenged, the phantom, the disguised, the aborted, the broken, the barefaced, the unattainable, the last time, the unreasonable, the fractured, the failure, the thump, the temptation, the fib, the pledge, the wish, the gone, the eclipse, the fabrication, the slut, the obsession, the illogical, the irretrievable, the rush, the snare, the inescapable, the lifeless, the incarcerated, the inconceivable, the mistake, the incendiary, the squandered, the mutable, the speechless, the filthy, the ongoing, the empty, the fallen, the earthworm, the custodian, the despair, the shadows, the first sight, the defector, the forfeit, the descent, the abandoned, the lament, the impasse, the refusal, the deserter, the spy, the unhinged, the insurmountable, the displaced, the unforgettable, the overlapping, death, desire, mutation, dispersal, fusion, devastation, orgasm, augmentation, alchemy, alcoves, garlands, bark, feet, olives, women, carved, in various stages of motioning.

Some Say the Devil Is Dead

NIDHI ZAK/ARIA EIPE

In 2008, Marcella Beccaria, curator of the Castello di Rivoli Museo d'Arte Contemporanea, commissioned a solo exhibition by celebrated artist Roberto Cuoghi. *Šuillakku* – as the show was to be titled – would represent lamentations for the fall of the ancient Assyrian city Nineveh. The pièce de résistance was a sculpture of Pazuzu, a fiendish demon of evil spirits and keeper of frigid winds which were thought to bring blight, famine and pestilence. The Met Museum's description of Pazuzu offers: 'He stands on two legs and has human arms ending in claws with two pairs of wings, a scorpion's tail, a snake-headed erect penis and a horned, bearded head with bulging eyes and snarling canine mouth.' Cuoghi's nineteen-foot-tall Pazuzu dominated the third floor above the entrance to the castle in Turin, a towering threat keeping watch over the unwitting visitors.

Cuoghi recalls an incident towards the end of the exhibition at the Castello, when he set about trying to transport Pazuzu to London. The statue was to be displayed on the roof of the capital's Institute of Contemporary Arts – 'so the demon from Mesopotamia had to wait for the permission of the Westminster Council, Royal Parks and Crown Estate, the Office of the Queen. After a week of silence, an objection arrived: 'Obscene'. They requested crotch photos and the measurements of the demon's penis, and everything had to wait three more weeks. No one had heeded one obvious particular: 'Pazuzu is not a classical nude,' Cuoghi said.

Fifteen years later, a historic town in County Clare seems to have stumbled across its own incarnation of Cuoghi's Pazuzu: the statue of a púca. Conceptualised by sculptor Aidan Harte, it draws on Ennistymon's equine heritage as the centre of an annual horse fair. Harte's design was selected in a competitive process through open tender. But when plans for the sculpture were unveiled to the public, it drew conflicting opinions ranging from beautiful and fantastic to sinister and grotesque, eventually gaining a niche notoriety when a local priest denounced it as a pagan idol.

The grotesque – a word which derives from the ruins of Domus Aurea, Emperor Nero's unfinished residence, owing to the corridors and rooms nicknamed caves, or grottes, where these frescoes were originally housed – is a style that often elicits unease, straddling the line between what critic Tim Smith-Laing terms 'a playful aesthetic and something that feels far more threatening'. Harking back to animistic rituals and the worship of idols, it situates human belief in a space outside – often before – religion. A key characteristic of the grotesque in art is its apotropaic function: employing the monstrous to protect against even greater evil. Pazuzu, for instance, was noted for his ability to ward off the malicious influence of the fiercest Mesopotamian chimera Lamashtu, a blood-sucking, flesh-eating, child-slaying demon. Likewise, in regional variants of legends of the púca across Ireland, the creature has been known to intervene and rescue humans from the curse of wicked spirits or terrible accidents.

Formally trained in classical sculpture at the Florence Academy of Art, Harte admits he would have been the first person to call his work grotesque. In his practice, he employs a technique known as écorché – 'flayed' or 'skinned' – in which the figure is sculpted without skin in order to reveal the bones and musculature underneath. This remarkable physical detail, coupled with a human stance and expression, gives Harte's Púca a resemblance to our species that perhaps accounts for the more disquieting effect the hybrid horse-man evokes for some. Harte speaks of a sort of spirit that animates his figurative sculptures: 'There comes a stage where there's a personality in the room other than yourself – it has its own charisma or its own presence, menace or humour. That's the stage when I usually walk away from a sculpture because then it has become something. Those are the most powerful sculptures – they seem to have a presence of their own.' Cuoghi talks about his art similarly, skirting a question concerning his relationship to his work with the response, 'I cannot say that I love my work, because it isn't that kind of emotion. It's like raising an animal that could eat you. I wouldn't know what to call that sort of affection.'

While the púca is rarely portrayed as a man-eating monster, a distinction reserved more appropriately for its counterpart the each-uisce, it remains a mythological highlight of Irish folklore, engendering a curious affection among its champions. A mischievous spirit, it can be, by turns, both malevolent and benevolent in its intentions. Accounts of its characteristics vary: it could appear with black or white fur, as a goat or a horse, rabbit or raven, wolf or cat, fox or dog, even a wild colt in chains. What is common to all accounts is that it is a shape-shifter, with the ability to assume human form and, perhaps more profoundly, the power of human speech. On 1 November, the day of the púca, it is believed to behave as an oracle, patiently prophesying the future for all those who approach for its advice.

This correlation of malign manifestation with guardian spirit tends to find expression most evidently, in the grotesque, through the gestures of the limbs. In Pazuzu's case, the deity is always shown with its right hand raised, either as a blessing or a warning – 'an imperative, like vade retro, to cure or to protect oneself.' Cuoghi remembers a group of Japanese tourists taking photographs in front of the Pazuzu, smiling, with their hands raised: 'It seems like they had misunderstood the position [of the sculptural gesture] as a wave of the hand,' he says, noting the resemblance to the Japanese figure of the Maneki-neko – a ceramic cat with a raised paw often displayed at the entrance of a space to attract good fortune. Misinterpretations in the meaning of gestures frequently occur when translating the divine and the demonic across cultures and time, such as the case of the Egyptian child god Horus, appropriated by the Greeks as Harpocrates. Images of Horus depicted him with his finger resting on his chin – its tip just below his lower lip – the hieroglyph for child, which the Greeks mistook to be a gesture of silence, so Harpocrates became the god of silence and secrets in the Hellenistic pantheon. Harte's Púca's hands are jovially clenched into fists, but the artist encourages people to rub its big toe to invite good luck.

This talismanic quality of the sculpture brings it closer to the concept of a personal amulet – carried close to the body, rubbed lightly over the skin – than institutional artwork. Harte's proposal for a life-size Púca, six and a half feet tall, was submitted in response to Clare County Council's call for a work of art that would perform as a tourist attraction, aiming to increase 'visitor dwell time' in the town. True to the maxim 'height is power in public art', Harte's Púca's stature itself created a bit of a stir. Yet perhaps this is precisely the scale at which the figure of the púca is most effective, a scale that does not detract from either its mystery or power. Cuoghi recognised this as well, using the original dimensions of the first millennium fifteen-centimetre-tall statuette of Pazuzu housed at the Musée du Louvre to recast the demon as a six-metre bronze. The artist justified his statue's commanding presence, that dominated the facade of the Savoy Castle, as congruent with the deity's purpose. 'Pazuzu is a watchdog,' he affirmed. 'The display case in the museum makes him fall asleep.'

Casting has currently been paused on the sculpture now colloquially referred to as the Púca of Ennistymon, and a decision on the follow-through or relocation of Harte's Púca sculpture has yet to be confirmed. In the meantime, a small bronze version – *Púca Beag* – is on display at the Sol Art Gallery in Dublin. Harte affectionately refers to his Púca as a figure of chaos. Fittingly, his own rendition of the trickster has a lightly crazed look in its eye, an intoxication reminiscent of the wild god Pan. The line in Harte's sculpture is gleefully kinetic; it revels in movement. For all the brouhaha it has created, its spritely appeal – that elusive, spirited presence – appears to remain undiminished. As I turn back at the door to catch its gaze, I can almost see the prankster pony gambolling off into the undergrowth, grinning.

A Swiftish Life

STEVEN METHVEN

The swifts arrive in Leipzig, as they do in every other central European city, in early May. From – or so it seemed – one day to the next, strips of empty sky, which bluely ceilinged rooms of street and building, became the busy highways of these creatures' passage. They appear each year in enormous numbers, a mess of darting bodies and joyous screeches, a cloud of happy disorder disguising geometric precision. From my balcony, I watch them for hours of an evening, my head tilted back until my neck hurts. Often, a small squadron of ten or so hurtles past in perfect formation, screaming gleefully. Close enough that I could reach out my hand and touch them, were they not there then gone so fast. Still, I'm satisfied enough to trace the parabolas and hyperbolas, the arcs and cissoids, conchoids and spirals of these lives Archimedean. The weather warms, the evenings lengthen, the swifts swoop in the sunset, and I recover.

The German word for the common swift is *der Mauersegler*. The first part – *Mauer*, which means wall – derives from the locations of their nests of spit and straw and other fragments plucked from the breeze, which cling gingerly to eaves, walls and church spires. The second part, *Segler*, can mean a sailor, as in a seaman, but also a sailer, as in a craft that sails. It is this second meaning that I prefer, taking it to honour the sense in which the tiny body of the bird exhibits both the fragility and the determination of a small boat at sea, each the unassuming master of an element infinitely more powerful than it. When I first learned this name, I added it to my list of those German nouns possessing a business-like matter-of-factness. Gloves, which are hand-shoes (*die Handschuhe*); the tortoise, which is a shelled-toad (*die Schildkröte*); the kitten, which is a cat-baby (*das Katzenbaby*); and the slug, which is a naked snail (*die Nacktschnecke*). Of course, I thought, in German something that seems to sail would be a sailer. Until I remembered that in English, a thing that is swift is called a swift.

In Bristol, where I spent the hard winter, the swifts have arrived too, though in numbers quite insipid. From the Clifton suspension bridge, whose length I measured in trudges those grim months, you might now see a splayed handful glide about the gorge below, filling their beaks on the wing with mosquitos, flies and, in the late summer, infant spiders travelling up and away by silky balloon. It is an odd inversion to view the birds' flight from above, rather than beneath, watching them skitter like fish on the muddy surface of the Avon instead of darting the gold between sun and eye. The angle is robbery, rendering their flight mundane and joyless, a perfunctory passage from one point to another. From the bridge, looking down, there are only straight lines. The spaciousness of the curve, its intrinsic expression of hope (it takes faith to go the long way around), is impossible from this Euclidian vantage; here, all lines chart the shortest route from this place to that.

On 8 May 1885, Sarah Ann Henley, twenty-two years old, walked a rough mile in a roughly straight line from her father's house in St Philips to the suspension bridge. It was just before noon when she arrived. Had it been a few hours later, she might have watched the first of the season's swifts glide the turbulent currents of a west-country spring. The morning was probably cool. Certainly, it was dry. It's natural to think that there is no way of knowing her precise state of mind when she stepped onto the bridge. The internal facts strike us as opaque, sealed away like a private nut rattling in a private shell, denizens of the realm of speculation rather than of knowledge. The external facts; these we can list. That she had been made distraught by receipt of a letter from her fiancé, terminating their engagement. That, some time before the letter, she had been furious enough about his conduct to upbraid him in front of an audience of his co-workers at the office of the Great Western Railway. That, at quarter-past twelve, reaching the centre of the bridge, she mounted the low barrier that existed then. That she swung her legs over and out into the air. That she dropped.

No way of knowing. Can't we know, though? Each of us, what it would take to make our bodies crash through seventy-five metres of nothing? Not a broken engagement, or a bad boyfriend;

not a ruined life or an emptied soul. Just a decision, a thought made rule: dive.

The swifts winter in central Africa. That's the way it's put, though no one knows exactly where. Their constant movement – they eat, sleep, mate in the air, landing only once a year for any length of time in Europe to raise their young – renders them difficult to track consistently. The air is their home, far above the treetops, and their range is without fixed boundary. Maps of their migratory journeys display only vague termini, shapeless blobs over the Congolian rainforest, Malawi, Mozambique. Of course, they winter nowhere. Our earthbound seasons are hemispheric perspectives the swifts know nothing of. Rather, they summer and summer, always swimming the sun, thousands of miles of it in a swiftish life. The travel, it seems, in a swift life, can be to the moon and back some seven times. Millions and millions – some seventy million each year – somehow finding their way here, there, back, forth, curlicuing the sky the alphabet of an endless, unreadable letter.

Some letters should remain unread. Five, arranged on a desk. Another, announcing the end of a love, and clutched like a one-way ticket to anywhere but here.

Sarah Ann Henley rolled from the bridge's barrier head first. Her body turned a full somersault as she dropped, an acrobatic tangle of cloth, hair, limb. The bridge was busy, its pedestrians battling the stiff breeze and unsteadied by the undulations coaxed from the concrete by the wind. Immediately, a crowd gathered at the spot vacated. Passers-by below stopped, craned their necks, pointed. And then, who can say: a circus trick, a miracle, a personal intervention by the laws of physics. Catching the updraughts from the gorge below, just as the wings of the summer swifts do, her crinolines puffed around her to form a petticoat parachute (*der Reifrockfallschirm*). That is how we know the day was dry. Her fall slowed considerably – 'like a leaf', a witness reported. Drifting, the crosswind altered her trajectory, not now directly down, but a diagonal around which she spiralled in ever-widening rings. A *spira mirabilis*. Eventually she came to rest, not eternally, not smashed dead on the surface of the Avon, but temporarily, sinking to her neck into the sticky, welcoming mud of its low-tide bank. She held his letter in her pocket.

The rattling nut in the shaken shell. Snatching herself from life, only to be snatched from death. Flatulently hoisted out of the embracing mud by her armpits, a kind of birth (is the obvious thing to say). 'Sarah Henley, 48 Twinnell Road', she stated when asked, still conscious though pale and dazed on the Gloucestershire bank. She broke no bones, but spent a long time in hospital recovering from the shock. Of what? Her own determination, her failure, her terrified awe at God's or fate's interference? *God sees the little sparrow fall.* While she lived to eighty-six, there is no record of her fall in Sarah's own words. Fall or flight? Fall turned into flight, though what is a fall anyway but, viewed from the right angle, a flight from one perch to the next, or to none?

The swifts, though expert fliers, are not immune to falls. Sometimes you'll come across one on a Leipzig pavement or balcony, killed by wall or window. Sometimes they are alive, a bird newly fledged who, landing to rest, learns that it does not yet have the power to take off from level ground. In the air, a swift appears to have no legs – a feature that defines the heraldic symbol called the Martlet, itself an older English name for swifts, which has in place of feet three feathery tufts. To see a grounded swift is to sympathise with the falseness of the diagram, as well as to understand the bird's scientific name: *Apus apus* – footless, twice, as though for emphasis. Their legs are stunted, slightly leathery nubbins from which emerge four toes, paired and splayed outwards, each of which bears a grappling claw. To pick one up is to feel the weight of barest existence, a whisp of fluff with thumping heart. But raise your arm, and stretch out your palm. Feel the fierce beat of scimitar wings, and an unexpected swirl of air, strong enough to disturb your hair. It goes. Some things are not made for this earth.

I had nothing to fear from petticoats. Low tides and muddy banks were another matter, and so on I winterly walked, back and forth, trying to map their precise location. The Avon, though, is irregular, its sands shifting from one day to the next. Nothing is stable. Only twenty-three years ago, new barriers were erected atop the ones from which Sarah Henley dove. Wire fences five feet high, topped with five parallel wires, stretched taut and sloping inwards. Still, some four people per year find their way through, and then through again to wherever they are going. My dreams contained, among the usual ephemera of sex and bears and water-logged books and coloured rain, bolt cutters. And Sarah Henley. Not her despair, nor her miracle. But the moment, again and again, when her torso teeters between earth and space, tips. Her fingers glide the concrete (the last surface, she realises, she will ever feel), and her body drops, and she thinks: *what have I done*?

I knew how she felt. The sensation turned my nights sleepless, something like vertigo, something like nostalgia, the aura of a migraine perhaps, flipping my stomach though I'd not moved at all. The same nut rattling and rattling in a different shell. Haunted by irreversibility.

They used to think that the screams of a swift were the souls of the recently dead, together on their final passage. A one-way group excursion to somewhere other than here.

One night, there they were: five unreadable, unread letters on the desk. The next morning, there they were, five unreadable, unread letters torn to pieces, a fate shattered in the bottom of a waste-paper bin. What passed in between? You can't know. No healed engagement, no bettered boyfriend; no salved life nor soul replenished. Just a decision, a thought made rule: don't.

When the swifts fly their long distances north or south, they fly as high as 10,000 feet. At that iced altitude, where lowered air pressure spaces oxygen molecules to breathlessness, they enter a state of half-life. Gliding torpidly aloft in the blue, this is where they sleep, their bodies reacting instinctively to the currents of the air, adjusting to its gives and takes, as yielding as aerial flotsam. Unconscious then, outside of themselves, other, waking only to life as they drift gradually downwards to the warmer, thicker air. I suppose the swifts do winter too. Not according to the position of the sun, but via a different disconnection.

At winter's end, I leave England. Walking the Clifton Downs

the day before, I find myself on the suspension bridge again. That's a lie. Finding myself on the Clifton Downs the day before, I walk to the suspension bridge again. At its centre, I mount the low, older barrier, across which Sarah Anne Henley swung her legs, and face the cage. And I spit. A weak, sad little thread of saliva joins my lip to it.

'Oi!'

In my willingness to be found always in the wrong, the boy on the bicycle is made an authority. I find myself wiping my mouth with the back of my coat sleeve, my face hot and an apology already shaping my lips. He stands beside me now.

'Like this, right.'

A sucking sound, from the nose, the throat, the lungs, three tugs at some internal mechanism, a head thrown back then whipped, and with the slightest whistle, a great silvery flob flies through the fence. It arcs, splays, spins, a ball then a whip then a star, flashing and falling, fading to glisten, gone. We watch its fall.

'Go on'.

His face? But an assortment of features adorning that joyous grin.

The last swift left Leipzig a few days ago. The evenings empty of their shrieks, as they do each early August. Probably that straggler is already somewhere over West Africa, tacking and slinging with guileless fidelity, tearing ribbons of sky. Now and again, of an evening, I imagine I hear one scream. But no, it's just some other city interjection – bicycle brakes, people having fun, the teething baby below, a tram connecting too closely with its guiding wire.

You can find online a picture of Sarah Henley. It is a typical Victorian photograph: poised, intense, emotionless. I look at it from time to time, searching those dark, unfocused eyes for something resolved, something relieved. An irreversible structure. Five months ago, I threw an excess part of myself into the Avon. It may grow back. And the swifts will return too.

Brave in Bed

BRECKEN HANCOCK

I take my phone to bed – my husband on one side, my cell on the other.

I face my cell.

■

It starts with a skim of scalp.

The cadaver of a Texan murderer who died of lethal injection was encased and frozen in gelatine, then ground down on the axial plane, one millimetre at a time.

Photographs of his 1,871 cryosections compile like leaves of a book; a stack of rectos; a secret turf of nerves (stubs of axons and dendritic miles); atrial chambers; a bog of colon; fat; furls of brain; and tendons, imprecisely milled, smeared across the surfaces.

■

He wasn't sliced.

In a university lab in Denver, a motorised, rotating disk of sandpaper scoured him away, turning him to frozen, cadaveric dust.

■

Each milling of his corpse revealed an aerial view of viscera – a slab of anatomical features – as, stratum by stratum, his head came open and utter darkness was amputated into light.

They shot photos of him, the remainder of him, of it, the rock-hard and shiny top of a stump that had once housed an appetite and an imagination.

■

I'm not moralising; I love looking.

These same layers of meat stack to make me.

■

He was a murderer.

To eliminate a witness during a burglary, he repeatedly stabbed a man and then shot the same man three times.

He was convicted and sentenced in Texas, where they put some kinds of criminals to sleep.

He ordered cheeseburgers for his last meal and then refused to eat.

■

FINAL MEAL REQUESTS

Ex.	Last Name	First Name	Date	Final-meal request*
63	Jernigan	Joseph	08/05/1993	Two cheeseburgers, French fries, tossed salad with Thousand Island dressing and iced tea (refused last meal).

* *The final meal requested may not reflect the actual final meal served.*

■

The prison chaplain pressured him to donate his body to science.

But he never knew that he'd be polished down, head to toe, for me to look at.

■

What am I looking at?

A body is atoms, a branching nothingness.

I flip through his leaves.

Where was he in here, in these pieces?

You know the *he* I'm talking about.

■

Sometimes I feel absolute, but not tonight.

Lying in bed, I release Joseph Paul Jernigan, the sixty-five gigabytes of his data, and the blue light of my phone back to the nightstand.

Dark tars the room.

Our humidifier pitches white noise over the bed and my accumulated slices of eyeball stare toward the ceiling.

Skin chafes against a snag in the cotton comforter.

■

It's the quality of the air.

I can't feel it but I can feel it, touching me.

Shadows against the plaster but – from here to there – air.

Some of it along my tongue and down my throat, packing me thick and wide and deep.

■

Consciousness has a wattage, but who controls the switch?

Who dims me down through ombré darkness, the substrative depths?

■

We need better linens.

IKEA's thread count is bullshit.

■

Through earbuds, I hear Tara Brach's meditation podcast.

Relax right down to the root of the tongue, notice how the mouth might fill with sensation: tongue, gums, teeth, lips.

To meditate is to apply attention to breath and body and one second of this activates a granular discomfort.

Sense the throat filling the neck.

I am atoms, a surge of overlapping dots.

Aware of the legs, the length and volume, so you're feeling from the inside out, right down to the feet, feeling the pressure, the warmth, the temperature, the aliveness inside the feet.

What is the body if not a stump of wet dust awakened temporarily and inexplicably into life?

Widening the attention, so you can feel sensations throughout the body, simultaneously.

■

My skull disturbs a pillow.

A micron slice of scalp crawls at the follicle.

Every epidermal electron strikes the sheets.

I can't sleep.

■

I wish someone would tell me what sleep is or how to achieve it.

Every night I come to this bed like someone thirsty who's gone to the sink.

■

I want to show up here and drink, ingest the molecules of the room, knit the ingredients of darkness into my darkness, quench what's tired in my cells, and come away sated.

But the ritual is more spell than transaction.

There's no material here to slake exhaustion – I've slid my spent body down into blackness only to be stormed by the spiny debris of consciousness, the mind's assault of the mind.

Nerves snarl; the heart beats at the thorax from beneath.

One by one the hours dissolve, and I feel their loss as grief.

■

I spend the night in the amplified consciousness of a fool.

Google informs me that cells in the human body die and are replaced at varying rates – it takes six days to get a new cervix, two months to get a new trachea, ten years to get a new skeleton.

Neurons – the cells that make up the nervous system, spinal column and brain – don't die, but all of the atoms in the human body, including those that constitute neurological cells, turn over.

The top thirty layers of the epidermis are expired cells that slough off and become household dust.

I touch my husband's naked back, there, where he's already dead.

■

Sometimes my husband wears pyjamas, but tonight his skin lies long beside me.

I put my forehead against his spine and smell laundry detergent and farts venting up from under the sheets.

A song creeps into my head and spirals on repeat – a mechanical, nasal melody from a computer game I played in my twenties:

I love you warm baby, warm baby, I love you.

I want to wake him for sex, but he has an early meeting.

In protecting his sleep, I feel virtuous and heroic – he should thank me.

Maybe I'll wake him for that.

■

I don't wear pyjamas because I'm not ten years old.

■

I turn to Maria Konnikova's series of articles on sleep in the *New Yorker*.

Here's what's supposed to happen when you fall asleep.

Your body temperature falls, even as your feet and hands warm up . . . circadian clocks throughout your body synchronize.

Melatonin courses through your system – that tells your brain that it's time to quiet down.

Your blood pressure falls and your heart rate slows.

Your breathing evens out.

You drift off.

▪

In our waking lives, my husband and I divide administrative and household labour.

He cooks and decides where things go in the shed.

I list shit on Kijiji and launder the piles of textiles that must advance from hamper to basement to closet every Saturday.

I chose the tog of this duvet; I'm too hot and have only myself to blame.

▪

With the largest toe on my right foot, I pin a bit of gravel to the mattress and drive it, one millimetre at a time, over the sheet.

▪

I watch the ghost of a window behind curtains, a wedge of orange light under the door, red minutes counting themselves to morning.

My breasts run across my ribs like raw egg.

I recline in a pool of thighs.

■

Netflix, too, is on my phone.

Over the edge of the bed, on dim, I watch billionaires gesture at earth they gutted with dynamite so their homes would look in tune with the landscape.

Caroline Quentin slumps back across a white duvet in cave-like guest quarters: *I love this bedroom, this so secrety bedroom.*

The designer and owner of the home, Bjarne Mastenbroek, laughs: *That's why architecture's not so important; it's the bed linen.*

■

Sleep's realities factor little in our cultural imagination: even television bedrooms set in Florida swell with winter duvets as heavy as weighted sensory blankets.

I guess we're all just trying to get cosy.

■

And I'm certain sleep is something I could achieve if only I were elsewhere.

In this way, sleep's like writing – in either case, it's the room's fault I'm not relaxed or productive.

▪

Two cats are killing each other for territory in the street.

They scream like babies with bad dreams.

▪

I get up to go pee.

We have a couple of kids asleep in other rooms, two little cuts I bleed through.

I slip past their closed doors, trying not to wake them.

The bathroom window leaks so much streetlight it could be day and, whatever's happening out there, the world wants to fall asleep and forget it.

My phone vibrates; Dad, Egypt Standard Time, says things are going well on his cruise.

▪

I'm on the cold seat past the point of pissing to finish Alison Gopnik's chapter on waking consciousness and sight.

Almost all studies of adult consciousness involve focused attention and a narrowly defined task – when we attend to something it's as if we shine a beam of light on it that makes all its details more vivid.

The book glows up off my palm and, behind my eyes, the city of lucidity remains lit.

■

Babies' consciousness is less like a spotlight and more like a lantern – *a vivid panoramic illumination of the everyday* – which adults sometimes experience in meditation, in mania, or when falling in love.

The mania of insomnia explodes surfaces into particulars – I love how this bathroom provides evidence of my existence everywhere: I chose the quartz, walnut, chrome and tile.

The Zen master Shunryu Suzuki called lantern consciousness *'beginner's mind', the mind as it is uncontaminated by expertise.*

I'm reminded of my kids, just through that wall, dreaming their big, naïve dreams.

■

Now I'm thumbing through photos of the kids because nostalgia is the most potent form of love.

■

I hate being awake while my family sleeps.

All day, all I want is some quiet to myself.

But at night, in the silence of the house, I feel nuts.

I'm alive and infused with consciousness and I could do anything to them.

And what's coming is coming.

■

Eventually I set down my phone and pull up my panties.

I drink from the faucet, then look out from my head into the mirror.

Time is hard to observe as it's passing, but then it's there, obvious, all at once.

Fuck, my face.

Anatomists refer to eye sockets as orbits, the emptiness in the skull that holds planets.

Space has weight, a shape and a power.

There's gravity beneath my eyes.

■

This story of sleep emerges from lack.

Shivering in my underwear, I close my eyes against myself: if consciousness so fundamentally enlists sight, shouldn't falling asleep be this easy?

But, no; there's an underside to seeing.

In 1995, an issue of my dad's *Scientific American* arrived at our door containing a picture encoded in a field of overlapping dots.

You can still find it, and the description of how to decode it, on the internet.

■

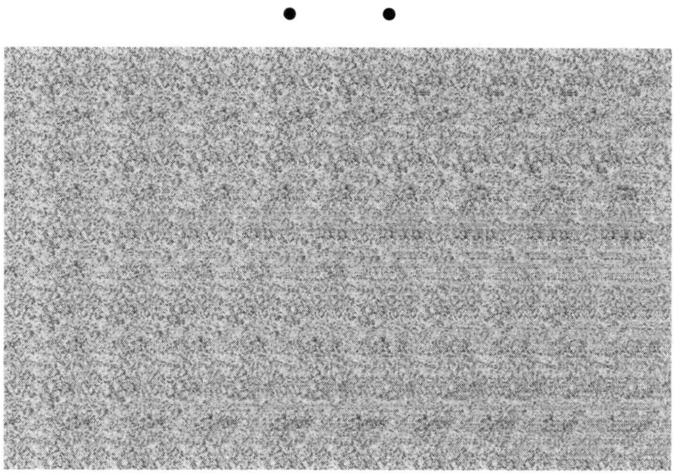

Just cross your eyes until the two black dots above this image become four.

Then, through luck or will, make the two central dots of your hallucination coalesce, until only three spots remain.

Take an aspirin.

Focus on the middle dot.

When it is clear and unmoving, slowly bring your eyes down over the picture.

■

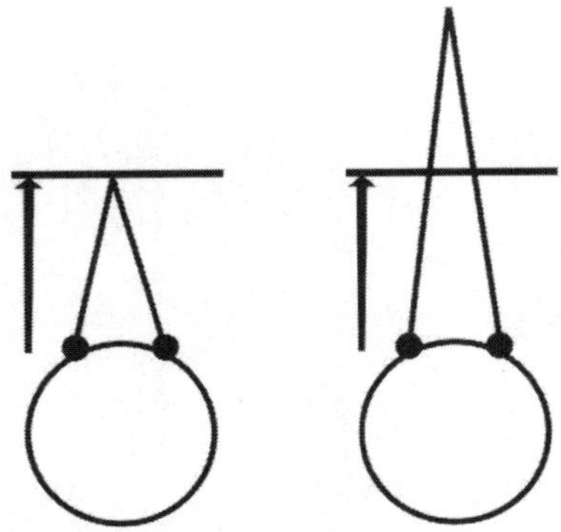

Normal viewing versus wall-eyed viewing: To see the image encoded in a stereogram, the eyes must covercome their automatic co-ordination between accomodation (focus) and vergence (angle).

■

Maybe sleep demands a wall-eyed consciousness.

To 'look' – not at but through.

To fall through.

■

When I come back to bed, he's on my side.

I growl.

In sleep, he's single: absence from our bed is my erasure.

The mattress feels hot to the touch and I shove him over with both palms.

There's no one to talk to: his back curves away from me.

Sleep is sovereignty.

■

Ever since giving birth to the kids, one or another of my hips or shoulders or limbs will go numb.

I try the foetal position on my right.

I try savasana, then a pillow between my knees on my left.

I splay on my stomach, then flip to the other side.

■

Also, Kathy really pissed me off this weekend.

I compose scripts for the next time I see her.

Choke on the mixed results of your own choices.

Your dog is the only audience for your stories.

Look at your panty line, you asshole, and despair.

■

It's a demonstrable fact that lying quietly in a dark room dials up the pain metre.

There's a questionnaire in my inbox, forwarded by a friend with sleep apnoea.

How much sleep did you receive last night?

How often have you lain awake because of pain?

On the diagram, shade in any painful areas.

Put an X where you hurt the most.

■

Some people are born with an inability to feel pain.

For those with congenital analgesia, sensation is normal except for temperature – for example, they can register the pressure but not the warmth in touch.

They often die as children after failing to report harm or illness: fatal burns, for instance, are common.

I've also heard that some people don't get anxious or depressed.

But I don't think it's life-threatening.

■

Every night I come to this bed like someone thirsty who's gone to the sink and then can't remember what brought her there.

I turn toward my cell.

■

Those who sleep less than eight hours a night die sooner.

Children need thirteen hours a night to be happy.

Sleep less, live longer.

Infants who die suddenly do so in their sleep.

Sleeping more than nine hours can have some pretty scary consequences.

Sleep disorders have major consequences.

Those who sleep less than four hours will suffer consequences.

Cardiovascular disease, obesity, depression, diabetes and even dementia can develop.

Twenty-one per cent of fatal car accidents are caused by a sleepy driver.

Regular oversleeping means a forty-four per cent increased risk of death.

You won't believe the amount of sleep that could kill you.

■

Waiting to die must awaken beginner's mind – that childlike state of consciousness uncontaminated by expertise.

I mean, what are we less accomplished at than death?

■

We imagine sleep to be an incubating form of death, and we want to die in our sleep as though the transition were trivial, from one oblivion to another.

But sleep and death are related only from the vantage of consciousness: to the conscious mind, any loss of control is cessation.

■

Unless you're on death row.

Then, I can only assume, any conflation of sleep with death would reveal itself to be absurd.

■

That night, the atoms in the prison's bars exchanged places with those in the air and some became flesh and some peeled away.

And in the panoramic illumination, I think he could see it.

■

Our bodies are made to feel pain and it's coming.

■

The prison chaplain convinced him to give his flesh to science, but he didn't know that he'd be sanded down, one millimetre at a time, for me to look at.

What am I looking at?

Tissue and blood and what looks like flattened mushrooms and bits of sky and emptiness where he was and what can never be photographed again.

■

To know the body, we defile its darkness.

To look – at it, through it – we open it, admit space and light.

■

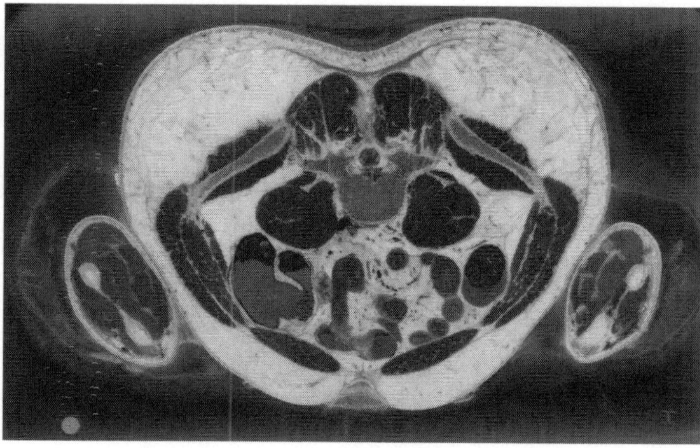

■

Joseph Paul Jernigan, your hamburgers are ready.

■

It turns out insomniacs sleep more than they think they do – misjudging how long it takes to fall asleep and how often waking occurs throughout the night.

They can confuse dreams with waking conscious thought.

■

We mistake being asleep for being awake.

Notes

- The National Library of Medicine describes its Visible Human Project (www.nlm.nih.gov/research/visible/visible_human.html) as such: '[The Project] has created publicly available, complete, anatomically detailed, three-dimensional representations of a human male body and a human female body. Specifically, the Visible Human Project provides a public-domain library of cross-sectional cryosection, CT and MRI images obtained from one male cadaver and one female cadaver. The Visible Man data set was publicly released in 1994 and the Visible Woman in 1995.'
- David Brown's article 'The Visible Human Project: A Slice of Life' (*Washington Post*, 13 January 1999) provided descriptions that were influential to ideas throughout: 'All of the body's functions arise from parts that are packed solid and working in total darkness. It's a revelation no less astonishing for being obvious. People who want to work inside this universe are faced with an ironic truth. They must violate the body's natural order before they can understand or repair it. The first task of the anatomist and the surgeon is to create space and admit light.'
- Joseph Paul Jernigan's final meal request, along with the final meal requests of other death-row inmates, was originally posted on the Texas Department of Criminal Justice's website. While this information has since been taken down, it was archived on 2 December 2003 at the *Internet Archive: Wayback Machine* (web.archive.org/web/20031202214318/http://www.tdcj.state.tx.us/stat/finalmeals.htm). The data's donor was Alexa Crawls, the AI developed by Amazon.
- Part of the line 'along my tongue and down my throat, packing me thick and wide and deep' is plagiarised from Souvankham Thammavongsa's

poem 'Sea' (*Light*, Pedlar Press, 2013). Lines 11–14 read: 'Then pack your lungs thick and wide and deep / with all of this / and go out there, there, where you think / you belong'.

- Tara Brach's website offers many free, guided meditations, including the one quoted in this piece. Passages here are taken from *Meditation: Natural, Open Awareness* (www.tarabrach.com/meditationnatural-open-awareness/).

- Lines enumerating the turnover rate of the body's cells and atoms were inspired by an interview with neuroscientist David Eagleman conducted by Lulu Miller for the podcast *Invisibilia* ('The Personality Myth' 24 June 2016). A Google search provided many additional details, most importantly from scientists Ron Milo and Rob Phillips' website *Cell Biology by the Numbers*, 'How Quickly Do Different Cells in the Body Replace Themselves?'.

- Maria Konnikova's description of the body's process toward sleep is from her article 'Why Can't We Fall Asleep?' (*New Yorker*, 7 July 2015).

- The reference to The World's Most Extraordinary Homes features a snippet of conversation from Season 1 Episode 4, 'Underground' (Netflix).

- Alison Gopnik's *The Philosophical Baby* (Picador, 2009) provided fruitful descriptions of consciousness, often leveraging sight as metaphor.

- Marguerite Holloway's article 'Secrets in Stereogram' (*Scientific American*, January 1995) is still available through the magazine's online archives. Copyright for the stereogram in Holloway's article, however, is not available; the proxy included here is courtesy of Easy Stereogram Builder (www.easystereogrambuilder.com).

- The images illustrating aligned vergence and wall-eyed convergence are copies of those found within the Wikipedia entry for 'Autostereogram' (en.wikipedia.org/wiki/Autostereogram). Most of Wikipedia's content, including these images, is available through Creative Commons: Attribution-ShareAlike 4.0 International. However, the anonymous artist/author notes that these were adapted from images in Stephen M. Kosslyn and Daniel N. Osherson's *An Invitation to Cognitive Science* (1995: page 65, figure 1.49).

- Most of the questions in the sleep questionnaire were drawn from a set of documents sent to me by a friend. However, the line 'How much sleep did you receive last night?' is from Nick Drnaso's graphic novel *Sabrina* (Drawn & Quarterly, 2018).

- Image from the Visible Human Project courtesy of the United States National Library of Medicine.

- Suzanne Buffam's *A Pillow Book* (Anansi, 2016) initially inspired this piece. Especially relevant is Buffam's discussion of insomnia: 'If an insomniac claims to drowse two or three fitful hours on her pillow, studies find, she has probably passed, in perfect peace, at least twice that time' (p. 81). See also Andrea Peterson's article 'You May Be Getting More Sleep Than You Think' (*Wall Street Journal*, 13 July 2015).

Club Oblivion

LIAM CAGNEY

As Indrani and I sweep up the charred-black staircase past a precipitously tottering woman, and as we hand our coats and bags to the tattooed *Garderobe* worker, and as we slip into a dank graffitied toilet cubicle, then, buzzing to at last be here, sweep back downstairs into the bar, slipping through the chest-to-chest throng, all leather and beards and babble, I have no inkling of the paranoia into which, like a slobbering dog falling into canal slime, my night will plunge, because for now, as I glimpse Indrani's complexion lit up George Grosz red, we are completely intoxicated by Griessmuehle's carnival, the club girls in glitter-ball face masks, the sweating bears, the spilt drinks and music, a pandemonium that, after the quiet unreality I've endured recently alone in my high-rise flat, feels like a happy dose of unbridled realness.

■

It's January 2020. And when, after weeks of prevarication, I finally decide that, yes, I *will* go to Griessmuehle's closing party, to the weekend-long closing party of one of Berlin's most beloved nightclubs, the first thing I wonder is what I should wear. Should I daub my lips purple again and rock up in my black and white stripes? Or, since I'll be going with my new girlfriend Indrani, should I instead wear the headdress she bought me, orange and green, with a string vest and silk floral shirt? An outlier is my fetish gear – mesh, dog collar – but although it's a queer party, fetish isn't Cocktail d'Amore's vibe, and although you want to be unique as you dance in the abandoned industrial units, you also want to fit in.

Like the butterfly effect, where a red admiral's wing-flap in the Caribbean invariably causes a devastating hurricane in the Outer Hebrides, one incorrect item of clothing at Griessmuehle's Cocktail d'Amore closing party might destroy my whole weekend. And Griessmuehle's closing party isn't just any party; it's a historical event, so you want to be dressed right. In our images of history, fashion's the unsung hero; without fashion, Napoleon at the Brandenburg Gate would have ruined his Prussian conquest by wearing fluffy pink galoshes; and had JFK, rather than a tailored suit, worn an Aran jumper and sandals with socks, his famous *Ich bin ein Berliner* speech would be long forgotten, remembered if at all as an embarrassing low point for our species. Such are my wild thoughts as, having confirmed, after depressed months laid up ill, that I will indeed have one last dance at Griessmuehle, I think about what to wear.

Perhaps Oscar Wilde's quip – *it is only shallow people who do not judge by appearances; the true mystery of the world is the visible, not the invisible* – is for you just that, a pretentious quip. But in the endless midnight of a party like Cocktail d'Amore, the deepest can truly become the skin.

■

A gay-nightlife staple, Cocktail was founded in 2009 by the Italian DJ and production duo Giacomo Garavelloni and Giovanni Turco (AKA Discodromo) with Berghain resident DJ Boris. 'Our taste was Italo, disco, house and, in general, music that would create some emotional reaction,' Discodromo told me. 'No other queer clubs or parties were offering this music. So together with Boris, we decided to start our own night, mainly for us and our friends who felt the same way about the music offerings from the club dance scene.'

Cocktail started off in a basement on Ritterstraße in Kreuzberg, before subsequent peregrinations around Berlin took in, writes Daniel Wang, 'a former brewery in Rollbergstraße . . . Chez Jacki on the Spree riverbank . . . a trashy, non-descript storefront hidden between sixties Plattenbau apartments and the Kino International, and an odd farmhouse-like structure behind the Hamburger Bahnhof'. Having arrived at Griessmuehle, a former factory in which Garavelloni and Turco installed a high-end sound system, the monthly party seemed able to end its wandering, finding a lasting home.

Cocktail's musical aesthetic is hybrid, open, playful, filthy, intense, self-subversive: in a word, queer. In the *Wintergarten*, you might hear Alex from Spain blasting out 'Relight My Fire'; in the main room, Discodromo spinning some indefinable psychedelic melange; in the smoky cosmic hole, Trent playing slow, narcotic crunk; then, in the garden, as dawn's rays glimmer through the branches, Daniel Wang spinning as an *aubade* Tomita's kitsch electronic synthesizer arrangement of Ravel's *Boléro*. 'We still book unknown talents we get excited about and try to create a unique yet very varied sound that some by now call the "Cocktail sound", unable to put it into a specific genre or defined box,' Garavelloni and Turco said.

Psychedelic-cum-pornographic graphics courtesy of Pindar Andriopoulos have been there since Cocktail's first flyer – a bouquet of roses made of cocks. Cocktail d'Amore's record label hosts productions by the likes of Discodromo and Sfire (Jeffrey Sfire and SOPHIE). For me, the track that distils Cocktail's vibe is 'Sfire 1', a sweet and driving party track with vocals by Marcela, electroclash meets Italo, light-headed and wistful and childlike, and now, since SOPHIE's death, almost unbearably bittersweet.

▪

When Saturday night enfolds us in its mysterious embrace, it's wet and dark and grim as only East Berlin in deep winter can be. On the tram to Indrani's Moabit flat, as I pass the hulking Plattenbauten apartment blocks at the Platz der Vereinten Nationen, I pass the time reading about Griessmuehle online. Located in the district of Neukölln, Griessmuehle is housed in a former grain mill (hence the name). Industrial units, railways lines and a canal insulate it from the outer world. Grain silos stand erect in rows or lie prone with revellers having climbed inside them. Wooden decking stretches away through sparse trees, which men climb up for shenanigans. Campfires are started; heart-to-hearts happen. The canal flanks the site like a moat, a ballast against reality – until now.

There isn't much you need to know about Griessmuehle's eviction. Briefly: the club is on a lease; the property-developer owner decides it's time to kick the shabby clubbers out to give way to the predictable generic hotel/office spaces/*exciting retail opportunities* – reality. Berlin's Club Commission and politicians step in as mediators, and after 45,000 people sign a petition and Neukölln's mayor speaks out, a compromise is reached: the site will be bulldozed, but the mooted *exciting retail opportunities* will become instead an *exciting cultural opportunity* (corporate sleight of hand); meanwhile, Berlin's politicians will help to find Griessmuehle a new home, supposedly (says the rumour mill) a site in the austere eastern district of Lichtenberg. I live in Lichtenberg, in a modest apartment on the twentieth floor of a GDR tower block with decades-old lino floors, a knackered sofa and a dizzying view of other Soviet high-rises stretching away to the horizon.

■

Janelle Monáe sings from the speakers and anticipation clasps my stomach as, in the bedroom of her flatshare, Indrani tells me about the performance-art piece she's writing. It's a spoken essay about her Indian grandfather, she says, the stern *paterfamilias* who during partition moved the family from India to New Jersey. Indrani's performance piece is about how in his patriarchal shadow the ties between his three daughters came undone; it's about how patriarchy sets women against each other.

Indrani was raised by her white father's family in North Carolina. She sometimes got to visit her mom in the Detroit projects.

'Two-thousand words. Now I have to memorize it. But I have my B2 German exam the same week, and I'm worried I'm putting too much pressure on myself.'

I watch her apply blue lipstick at the mirror. We met months ago at a club night in Wedding and grew attached, two immigrant artists with *de rigueur* precarious jobs. That night was Indrani's birthday and on the dance floor she was impossible to miss, laughing in an elegant white gown and gold earrings. We danced and hooked up and spent a weekend together during which we listened to Princess Nokia and she told me about her *Fifty Dates of Grey* pamphlet and Cindy Sherman and the Berlin Diaspora Society she was trying to get going, a support network for Brown artists. Tonight she's opted for a silver space-age dress with blue lipstick; on her forehead is a jewelled bindi. Meanwhile, I'm on the floor rooting around in my suitcase like a dog.

Indrani pops the cap on her lipstick and purses her lips. 'What do you think?'

I look at this retrofuturistic space diva in Indian jewellery.

'Gorgeous. But lose the fake septum ring, babe, you don't need it.'

My answer makes us both self-conscious; I feel my cheeks glowing and I go back to looking through my clothes. 'At least I got us on the guest list tonight,' I say, changing the topic.

If at their least imaginative clubs are four walls and a ceiling for people to get fucked in, at their best clubs are stages in which new personas aren't simply possible but demanded. So, while I'm drawn to the music and only sporadically take in what's around me, Indrani spends her time looking at the hats and belts and shawls and wigs, absorbing the inventive looks in what is effectively an art space just as much as is some sterile Mitte commercial gallery.

Baudelaire described fashion as 'a symptom of the taste for the ideal which floats on the surface of all the crude, terrestrial and loathsome bric-a-brac that the natural life accumulates in the human brain.' Fashion, he said, was 'a sublime deformation of Nature, or rather a permanent and repeated attempt at her reformation.' I can get with this idea of dressing up as an insouciant act of freedom in a degraded world that always falls short of our ideals. A person dressed stylishly shows *esprit*, truth through artifice, as I'd learnt from my Galway girl friends years ago. And through style you can express your gender however you want.

Now, I lift from my suitcase the porcelain harlequin face I found in a bargain bin in Humana. I attach the enigmatic smiling face to a lanyard and hang it around my neck. Yes, this'll do; Complicious, I'll call her, this harlequin who looks like Kraftwerk's niece cross-bred with Ornacia from *Drag Race* season six. As if creating a collage, I stumble upon my outfit by accident: after Complicious, I dress myself harlequinesque.

I enjoy the lipstick's taste as my lips turn red and black. I enjoy my red and black chequerboard blouse with the lumpen shoulder pads. I enjoy my knee-high socks in red and black stripes, my black shorts, my leather bumbag, my face that, below my red head-dress, I powder matte white. As if virginal, free of vulgar identity, untainted, my face emerges anew: daubed white blotches, dragged black lines, a surrealistic white under a thick black X. But in inventing my face I erase myself, erase my face while retaining it spectrally. In clubbing at Griessmuehle, in making myself art, isn't that ultimately the freedom I desire – death?

I've always felt alien to myself. Yet that ridiculous existential scenario – *always driven to seek and fail finally to become identical with yourself* – can be flipped into a liberation. Your self becomes the open portal through which you step to find the unknown, clasping for it in the darkness of your insides, the darkness of the club space, this sealed-closed world. Yes, it's hard to disagree with Baudelaire when he writes that, deep within such night-time spaces, the clubber is 'quite within her rights, indeed she is even accomplishing a kind of duty, when she devotes herself to appearing magical and supernatural'.

I come back to myself. Indrani's yuppie downstairs neighbours are banging the floor with a broom. 'Ignore it,' she says, picking up her keys.

By now it's well past midnight, but before leaving her apartment we take a couple of photos. The last time we went to Cocktail was

Hallowe'en, and we took photos of Indrani in an elaborate Marie Antoinette garb with a thick bouffant, pink gown and guillotine-marked neck, and me in a furry waistcoat and bandana. This time, scanning my photo, Indrani looks uncomfortable. I look over her shoulder.

Yes, I look ludicrously camp.

■

Not being over-blessed with queer friends in Berlin, the first time I went to Cocktail, having heard about it by word of mouth, I went alone. And I gabbed to randomers and had fun. I still remember the feeling, down the line, at Cocktail's tenth birthday party, when in a dark and teeming main room, Boris dropped Patrick Cowley's 'I Feel Love' remix. Sweat-scented and balmy with body heat, the room lifted off. As Cowley's synthesizer solo grew ever more ludicrous, hands threw silhouettes on the rainbow lights; two men made love; a hand-standing Italian woman tried not to topple over; the state of play was friendly, gay, delirious, and I felt like I'd been transported back in time to NYC's Paradise Garage circa 1980.

'It's a disco that absolutely blew my mind,' the artist Keith Haring said of the Paradise Garage, adding that it was 'nothing like other gay discos. . . . It's the closest thing to being at a Grateful Dead concert, except that it wasn't this hippie thing, but taking place in a totally urban, contemporary setting. The whole experience was very communal, very spiritual.' That sense of quasi-spiritual freedom – in style, behaviour, gender, music – gets at Cocktail's appeal. An Englishman spending a year in Berlin told me that Sundays at Cocktail had become his 'church'. You could be whoever you wanted without giving a shit about what anyone might think. Turco has said that, looking back, 'my life in Italy seems like a previous life. We both share this feeling, actually. When we moved to Berlin, it felt like being reborn. Completely. Sometimes I look back and I feel like I never had a life before Berlin. I was asleep, kind of.' Except now Griessmuehle is being demolished, and it's winter, and my bones are degenerating, and everything feels uncertain again.

▪

Shimmering Alexanderplatz appears outside the window as Indrani and I sit on the train heading west. As per my standard transit routine, honed over years of gruelling bus journeys to Donegal, I have ambient music on my headphones, *All Lanes of Lilac Evening* by Siavash Amini & Saåad. Now, reading online again about Griessmuehle's closure, the music inadvertently imbues everything with a mournful, almost melodramatically tragic air, all tape hiss and synth pads and arpeggiated minor chords – a growing sense of ennui, regret and carsickness. For light relief I switch to the Facebook event page and scroll the comments. There's a post from co-organiser Giacomo: *Fun game: post a sneak peek of your ultimate outfit(s) for the weekend! (we know many of you have been working on it since the announcement of the last cocktail emerge eheh).* As in the Bayeux Tapestry the figures unfurl: a bearded man in a tiger costume; a bespectacled nerd sporting a full body condom à la *The Naked Gun*; a Barbie doll, naked, tied to a pole by her heel-length blonde hair; a paunchy bearded man modelling a pink bikini. But a palpable sense of dread has seeped into the fun: like this bereaved woman in black drapes and a thick veil ('I'll be the grieving widow all in black lace whispering "*amore* . . ." between sobs'). I take off my headphones – the train is edging into Sonnenallee, our stop – and I show Indrani how the most reactions are for a humorous stock photo of an East Asian man wearing a medical facemask. 'Thank God you got us on the guest list,' she says, as we step out into the rain.

▪

'The guest list's been frozen,' announces the party's gatekeeper, a swarthy man in white robes; he delivers his harsh judgement with a bizarrely quavering voice. 'There's absolutely no space left in the club,' he tells us and the other disappointed guest-list hopefuls gathered in the rain before him, 'so you'll have to wait for people to leave.'

'How long?' I ask. Behind his handsome face and shrill Aussie accent, I remark the light-headed look of someone coming up on a pill. 'Minimum three hours. Join the guest-list queue back there,' he concludes, pointing a hundred lamentable yards back down the long alley.

How proud we were, and now how crestfallen now we

feel, trudging back along the queue's multitudes of gay men in colourful outfits and women with piercings, every further footstep a humiliating slap in the face, taking us away from this party of parties! Eventually we end up behind an Irish group sharing a bottle of rum, among whom I pretend not to notice the redhead Limerick woman who once Airbnb'd a room in my Alt-Treptow flatshare, and who brought all manner of druggy chancers back to our apartment from Griessmuehle, having noisy sex while I lay cooped up and miserable in the neighbouring box room.

'What'll we do?' I ask Indrani.

Her narrow eyes are dimming. 'I dunno, babe, not feeling so good. Think I'm getting a cold.'

'Will we go to that other place for a while, where Ashanti ran the karaoke night?'

'The one at Richardplatz? That closes at two-thirty,' she says, looking at her phone. 'In ten minutes. Sorry, babe. I know you wanted to go dancing for your birthday. We tried. What about another club? Is there one nearby?'

The mere thought of going to some lesser club when the last Cocktail is on is rancid, like going to the cinema to see a new print of *The Bitter Tears of Petra von Kant* and, finding it sold out, having to settle instead for *The Fast and the Furious VII*.

I get down on my hunkers and check that the two pills in my sock are still intact. Should we pop them here to pass the time? The alleyway is wet and dirty and voices babble from both lines, the long guest-list queue and the infinite one for normal punters. A woman emerges from the club, staggering boldly. 'Does anybody have a lighter?' she asks the queue. 'Do you have a lighter?' I shake my head. A man leans over the steel barrier with a lighter and she pushes back his hand: 'Just because you are good-looking, doesn't mean I must talk to you.'

Everything becomes messy.

I drift.

In my mind a dream image flashes up: bodies in plumed Venetian masks, queuing in an alleyway; queueing not for a club but for soup. It's the video for David Bowie's song 'Fashion'. In a New York City dance studio, an African-American woman in a leotard directs people to imitate Bowie's gormless gestures, before snippets interrupt from fake TV ads for amphetamines. The video's a collage of nonsense, lacks any semblance of narrative, and it snatches victory from the maw of defeat. Reduced to attitude and pose, Bowie generates a sense from his material that couldn't pre-exist that material. This is exactly what I love in fashion – *the unforeseen made necessary* – the liberating trust in surfing the wave of one's imagination; life not as a set pattern but as an open experiment.

My reverie breaks. 'Time for evasive action. Stay here, I'm going to blag it.' I stride purposefully to the top of the queue, where the burly Turkish-German bouncer is letting in people who already have a wrist stamp. I gesture to the Asian-Australian gatekeeper in his white robes. Brandishing my phone, I explain that I'm a writer and, look here, I wrote this piece about Cocktail d'Amore for the *Guardian* and, you know, I might write about tonight's party, but I'm not able to stay on the whole night, just a few hours and—

'Oh, why didn't you say so . . . You're not *guest list*, you're *press list*.'

With relief, I dash back and grab Indrani. 'Busy night,' I say cheerily to the robed man when we return, who looks like he's trying to stay on top his jackhammer heartbeat. He smiles weakly and nods – 'One last time' – then, giddy with excitement, we're inside under red lights.

▪

At this point you might have to bear with me, reader, because it's later in the night, and everything's blotchily cartoonish.

I can't take my eyes off this lanky, haughty woman. She's dancing on a platform near the DJ box and she's yellow-skinned and femme. She's wearing an airy Twiggy dress and Holly Golightly sunglasses and she sets one platformed shoe before the other, one platformed shoe before the other, four-square, rhythmic limbs, right-angled elbows, while dancing beside her, his toady squatness ridiculously complimenting her lank pout, there's a headless monster. He has a shrivelled green face set in his tummy and he jives and jives, a carefree Blemmyes, waving a pair of white rave gloves – quite touching!

Below the disco femme and the monster there's a gay couple in the early stages of an encounter. A smiling boy in a string vest and blue shorts reaches one arm towards the older bearded man's crotch. Then, out of nowhere, the boy's arm merges with the bearded man's penis. Their joint penis-arm extends, a writhing trunk, a rippling waveform, an autonomous third entity, in time to the music.

And here, hand in hand, stumble space-age Indrani and harlequin me, half mad, as my little smiling amulet Complicious dangles from my neck. Cocktail's main room is a throbbing shadow, a flickering scrum pounding with Hi-NRG music. The dark is interspersed with halogen strip lights. A huge pile of empty bottles lies in the corner. And it's buoyant. Most of the men are topless, a virtual-reality gay club painted by Breughel, wet paint oozing in the heat. Cocktail's main room is like a laboratory for masculinities. Men experiment with masculinity, push at its contours, rearrange their gender in perceptual shards. Military epaulettes and leather jockstraps, drag and butch, animal and vegetal – through fashion's doorway, all wind in dance.

The dance music fascinates. My over-analytic mind characteristically flies into action trying to figure out what genre it is. Techno? Too many motifs. House? Too lacking in melody and harmony. Psychedelic, anyway – hybrid, the sonic correlative of the paint on my cheeks, of the necklace's geometrical relationship with Indrani's left shoe, multiplied by the hour of the o'clock it is, divided by the inverse square root of my heartbeat's bpm . . . But wait, that screaming – is it? – yes, Suicide, Alan Vega mixed over these beats – so surprising and unsettling!

I tug at Indrani's warm hand and we slip through the ranks down to the back of the room. From the ceiling, angry orange lichen droops and blue bananas grow. Two men embrace in high-vis vests. Viscid like glue, a membrane of an enormous eyelid unfurls across the ceiling for several metres, a biomorphic banner, ebbing towards that teeming pile of empty glass beer bottles underneath the speakers, glinting in the flashing disco lights like an insect's compound eye.

Now before me there's a punk with blue skin and a green Mohawk. His single head has multiplied into three heads, and each head is stacked upon the other. The blue punk leaps into the air, three mouths agape, and in his topmost head's mouth, I now see, this blue freak catches wonderfully a dazzling pink laser beam that's shooting from a huge bust in the corner, a statue of a green-skinned bearded bear.

'It's like a sauna,' Indrani says, disrobing her silver dress. Dizzy and sweating, I hang its flying saucer sheen over some exposed piping on the back wall, as drops of cold water drip on me from a ceiling crack. 'Much better,' she smiles.

At the top of the room, flashing red and blue lights trace broken geometries. Past them flies a huge pair of hairy balls. The balls are autonomous from any phallus and body. The airborne balls shoot out billowing dry ice on the dancers below, a cordial emission.

Happy birthday, baby, Indrani's smirking blue lips mouth as, her hand clasping my gloved fingers, my eyes flick open. Two green femme cone-head aliens are beside her, conjoined twins in yellow lace knickers. Pulling me through the darkness towards her bra and jewelled bindi, Indrani presses my waist against hers, and I feel her warmth, and in my skimpy shorts, shorts through which she so crudely groped me earlier, I feel myself getting hard. Happily my white face and lipstick aren't a turn-off. Happily she's forgotten—

Languorously kissing Indrani's warm blue lips under the

bellowing speaker, I disappear out of my body through her mouth, at the back of this teeming squirming dancefloor, sluiced altogether from existence, vanishing in stars and nebulae, disappearing in comets through our bodily congruence, which I've so much missed this mentally ill winter, disappearing from my white face, my red- and black-painted lips and red headpiece until, brought back to myself again through a hard object under my shoe, I realise Indrani's not here. I'm standing on a man's foot and in dumb apology I gesture to his scowling boyfriend, like a pantomime.

■

The stronger the cut that a club effects with the outside world, the better the club is. Industrial ruins and non-functional architecture are best: they seclude, shelter, create exclusivity; and, when there are no windows, no sign of the sun rising or falling, they can allow clubbers to forget absolutely the outside world, the oppressive ferule of ever-ticking clock hands; to submit to play and glamour.

'Either the well was very deep,' Lewis Carroll writes, 'or [Alice] fell very slowly, for she had plenty of time as she went down to look about her and to wonder what was going to happen next. . . . Down, down, down. Would the fall never come to an end?' It can feel like this entering Griessmuehle. Having passed under a railway bridge and turned left onto a long alley, you walk for an age towards Griessmuehle's entrance along a kilometre-long stretch of concrete, Alice's well rotated ninety degrees and becoming a dirty inner-city catwalk. As you transition, you're granted at least a preparatory sideshow. Dishevelled club kids walk in the opposite direction, tender from their sleepless adventures, distraught or smiling crookedly.

So as Indrani and I, at 2 a.m. on the rainy night of Griessmuehle's closing party, walked down the long alleyway towards the club, a shadowy woman and man appeared enigmatically in the distance. They were like emissaries of a foreign land. The woman in particular, a drag queen in a crumpled cocktail dress, with blonde curls and a tiara, projected a regal air, all the more effectively seductive because of the exposed catwalk of her approach. Her wrangled regal head seemed a pre-taste of Cocktail: *you are entering an altogether different place.* Indrani and I approached the drag queen and her courtier companion, and I thought of how Proust's narrator describes, from the Paris opera stalls, gazing up in wonder at the spectacle of the Duchesse and Princess de Guermantes making their entrance: 'I had no doubt that their manner of dressing was peculiar to themselves, not merely in the sense that livery with red collar or blue lapels had once been peculiar to the houses of Guermantes and Condé, but rather as for a bird, where its plumage is not some added adornment of its beauty but an extension of its body. The way the two women dressed seemed to me like the snow-white or the many-coloured materialiation of their inner worlds' – inner worlds that exploded with wild gentleness in this Griessmuehle queen's dilated pupil, exploding to envelop us.

■

A plump bird woman with yellow plumage has fashioned a mask from a glitter ball, and she pushes past us as we lean on Griessmuehle's main bar, as the distant music pulses over babbling voices. I'm still waiting at the bar to get served. How long has it been?

Bodies bustle in the red light. Across the bar there's the bald lesbian anarchist from Berghain chatting to the bulbous man with a goatee who always wears a rubber suit. A huge bouquet of fragrant white lilies dominates the bar, lending to the impression of a canteen on an alien planet.

The barman with a black hood over his face and hardware chains around his neck has ignored me for twenty minutes, doling out shots and long drinks to every other fucked face. What's the problem? He's currently light-heartedly chit-chatting to two men to my right. Indrani wraps her arms round me.

'I feel like the music was better last time,' she says.

'I felt like we were in a film in there,' I reply.

'You already said that, babe.'

The man with a handlebar moustache, whom I spotted outside in the queue wearing a dinosaur hat (an elaborate homemade hat fashioned from a child's 3D dinosaur jigsaw) pushes past us. In my left hand I clutch Complicious' porcelain. Finally, through his hood, the barman stares me in the eye and, after I greet him in German and ask for two Vodka Mates, with faultless *Schnauz* (a distinctively Berliner show of contempt), he takes my money and throws the too-generous tip in the jar, deliberately without comment.

‘Heterophobe,’ I mutter grumpily as I hand Indrani her drink. ‘He just sees you as one thing.’

‘Well, the . . . he doesn’t know your . . . your persuasion,’ Indrani stutters hesitantly.

There’s awkward silence. Indrani avoids eye contact. Yes, of course we will have to discuss this. But why the fuck now?

The bar’s redness, Grosz red – my mind’s redness.

‘Look’, Indrani says, switching topic, pointing at nearby graffiti. ‘1UP. Remember their mural by your Treptower Park flat?’ Around the white trail of the 1UP crew’s tag, too impatient to await the club’s imminent destruction, grubby patches of moss have already begun sprouting, encircled by red admiral butterflies, which seem to be visibly multiplying.

‘Butterfly effect.’

‘I have to go pee upstairs,’ Indrani says, turning and walking.

As I follow her, a lingerie-clad man almost falls down the stairs on top of me, embarrassed as I catch his arm. Briefly we chat. When I look up, Indrani is gone.

■

Walter Benjamin spent years writing his endless *Paris Arcades* project. The discotheque concept also arose in Paris – in the 1950s, spreading to the USA in the early 1960s, an immersive social space with artificial lights and a disc jockey. To the extent that the discotheque is French in origin, and that its spread demonstrates capitalism’s standardisation of urban space, it’s a kind of twentieth-century cousin of the nineteenth-century arcades. Benjamin quotes a contemporary *Illustrated Paris Guide* on that urban novelty of the 1830s and 1840s: 'a new contrivance of industrial luxury . . . glass-covered, marble-floored passages', lit by gas lamps, linking shops on either side, 'so that such an arcade is a city, indeed a world, in miniature'. Which is not dissimilar to club spaces at their most ambitious; especially when, as in Berlin, they're literally housed in the ruins of commerce and industry.

The Parisian arcades for Benjamin showed how capitalist reality acts: instituting an artifice as if it were natural. 'With construction in iron, architecture began to outgrow art,' Benjamin wrote. Architecture here isn't innocuous and neutral, simply a passage you walk through. Architecture in fact articulates you as a subject; it insidiously tells you who you are, a capitalist consumer and little else. Here is the birth of our modern world. These miniature environments, so aesthetically dazzling, induce narcotic forgetfulness and, in doing so, they erase other possible worlds, till you altogether forget who you might otherwise have been. Eventually, there no longer is any outside. Alongside the nineteenth-century standardisation of public space came a concomitant, no less contrived domestic interior: 'The private citizen who in the counting-house took reality into account, required of the interior that it should maintain him in his illusions,' Benjamin notes.

As time went on, from radio to TV to 5G, information technology took up and exploded what we might call the immersive arcades principle. The local Parisian prototype was projected wholesale onto our global sensory environment. Actual (IRL) and virtual (online) alike, our mass-media world, as Marshall McLuhan said, exists recursively, ceaselessly iterating, propagating itself as a spectacle, a *de facto* work of art. (Nietzsche, in his notebooks: 'the world as a work of art that gives birth to itself'.) Phantasmagoria (*Phantasmagorie*) is the word Benjamin used to describe this homogenous society and how we experience its alienating pseudo-reality. The resonance with Freudian phantasy isn't accidental: to call the everyday a *de facto* artwork is basically to say we're in a waking dream.

Phantasmagoria: doesn't that suggest the surreal environment of a night-club space?

▪

I think of the club as a play-within-a-play, a phantasmagoria-within-a-phantasmagoria. A Berlin club can be like a deconstructed arcade.

Embroiled in the everyday weave, the stream of dead concepts and dead images, of faded ideas and bland repetitions, all of which stage-manage us unbeknown to ourselves, we might come to realise one night that, although there is no outside, we have the power within us to work the weave. With an artistic eye, at special times we can embody fashion, say, in a way that gently tears apart the dream-fabric smothering us. In such cases, as with the butch queen in lingerie I just bumped into on the stairs, dressing up positively expresses a more-real selfhood.

That club culture should owe so much to queer movements is no coincidence. Judith Butler talks about critical gender consciousness as 'how to work the trap that one is inevitably in'. Butler shows how, at a deep structural level, gender and sex norms generate and organise us as conscious subjects. Gender identity is pre-conscious: it's wed to architecture and fashion as the texture of our collective dream. 'Fashion,' Benjamin wrote, 'like architecture, inheres in the darkness of the lived moment, belongs to the dream consciousness of the collective.' Queer club people reformulate and refashion the world. Their club world simulacrum shows that the outer world was always already a simulacrum. No wonder at Cocktail I instinctively started wearing peculiar outfits: those outfits, I realised, put me in touch with a more real self.

For now, as I pass along Griessmuehle's charred-black corridors amid bedlam, dressed in my harlequin gear, it's as if I'm in a Brechtean version of the capitalist phantasmagoria: the stage set is broken; the lights, flickering; the general apparatus, exposed and about to collapse.

■

I wait for Indrani in the narrow upstairs corridor. Bodies and heads move in every direction. Duos and trios go about their night, eyes bulging; I hold Ornacia. This morning – could it be true? – I felt suicidal; hard to believe, I think, clutching Ornacia tighter. After all my drama about what to wear, most of the other men here are semi-naked, wearing leather harnesses, pearl necklaces. And after my weeks laid up depressed, how mad it is to be in this carnival atmosphere. I think about the drugs in my sock, pressed against my ankle, probably melted in mush. Beside me, passing out on his feet, a fucked man props himself up against the wall while his boyfriend asks him what he took (he can't remember). From over the archway leading back downstairs, someone tears away the green fire-escape sign, which is less concerning when you remember that the whole building is going to be destroyed in a few days anyway. The proximity to erasure gives everything a preternatural clarity.

I dash inside the dank urinals room, which, as in all Berlin clubs, is plastered in fly posters, and I pee beside two men who have joined forces to enable the semi-conscious one to piss. A gymnastic woman, pants around her ankles, backs up and tries to piss in the urinal, spreading her legs in an arch, bending down to the ground and doing a half-splits. At Berlin club nights women suffer from the fact that the cubicles are always clogged with groups doing drugs.

I leave the urinals and go into the bigger toilets to seek my silver-dressed girlfriend. But I don't see her queuing there, and she doesn't answer when I call.

'I need a new life,' says a woman beside me in the queue in denim jeans, *à propos* of nothing.

I've taken off my headpiece and feel all floppy-fringed frazzled Manila Luzon as I take in the woman's freckles and bulbous pupils. 'What's wrong with your life, dear?'

Shaking her head, she deflates me with a literal German reply. 'I am just joking.'

The dank toilets resound with white-noise babble. Where's Indrani? A woman behind me in the toilet queue says she was standing outside Griessmuehle for four hours, so I let her go ahead of me. And soon I'm at least thirty minutes here waiting for Indrani, or waiting for one of the drug clusters to vacate a cubicle, and chatting is the only thing passing the time.

From her jeans pocket the freckled coquette produces a pink tube. 'This stick is my only treat. Wanna see?'

'My lips already have lipstick, babe. But sure.'

I turn the lip balm over in my fingers, not entirely sure of what I'm meant to be seeing.

'That', she says, 'is my only make-up.' (She's wearing eyeshadow.) 'It costs forty euros for this one stick. It does not colour your lips in an artificial way but . . . helps the colour that your lips are already.'

I look at her moist round pink lips. I nod. 'An enhancer.'

She grabs it back and turns to a stoned-looking Hispanic guy to her left. 'He is no good. You wanna try?' He smiles lazily and she begins dragging the stick across his lips.

An oblique connection strikes me. Of course! All those pink faces I was seeing on the dancefloor, and now this pink embellishment . . . Weird . . . Does it mean something? . . . That I should – put some on?

Two muscular American men dressed in black are leaning against the closed cubicle doors. '*Deine Tätowierungen sind wirklich cool*,' the coquette says to one of them.

'Thank you,' he drawls, then looks at his toned bare chest. 'Yeah, let's see: Boston . . . London . . . Tokyo . . . and this one here I got in Berlin.'

'That one is best,' she confirms, touching his right bicep, on which is tattooed a tacky pseudo-South Asian frieze, a horribly crude pseudo-Kama Sutra scene showing Ganesh fondling a woman's bare breasts. 'But stay it like this,' she adds, 'do not overdo them. The blank spaces are just as important, so stay it like this.'

Am I just being mad or is something clandestine being communicated here?

'Isn't that sorta cultural appropriation?'

The coquette looks at me, then sneers at her new pal. 'Virtue signalling!'

Instinctively, for comfort I reach for the plaster mask round my neck.

Ah! It's gone.

'Fuck!'

'What's wrong?'

I clutch at my hair and look in vain at the filthy ground. 'I've lost something.' This is great. Now not only have I lost Indrani, I've lost Complicious. That mask isn't just a straightforward accessory: the white harlequin face, the red and black lips smiling, is my miniature, my homunculus, my ideal. With Indrani nowhere to be found, this second loss really makes me anxious . . . I feel exposed, like Dolly Parton losing her wig.

Everything's out of kilter, like a doctor's waiting room. A door swings open and a man in Dayglow yellow underwear strides past holding his phone, talking exuberantly on Facetime – he must have gotten a good report . . .

On the floor I see the coquette's chapstick in a puddle. As soon as I notice the pink stick, the puddle starts turning pink. A rippling mouth coalesces – two yellow eyes.

The freckled woman turns towards me her slim green irises. Her warm arm touches mine. 'Come, you need a shot?'

▪

No small part of my *Drag Race* infatuation is the joy in seeing people invent themselves – naming themselves, pouring themselves out, the joyous paradox of dancing queen Alyssa Edwards exaggerating and exaggerating that hair and eyeshadow artifice to reveal her authentic truth. Benjamin thought that, through dialectical analysis of modern Paris at its dreamworld's inception, he could show the roots of our modern alienation. But doesn't camp do the same thing – and with brio? For queer people, parodying gendered fashion norms – whether a cop's uniform or a prom dress and moustache – works the trap, tears the map.

Really, Clarice Lispector speaks for me when, in rhapsodic mode in *Água Viva*, she writes: 'I, anonymous work of an anonymous reality only justifiable as long as my life lasts. . . . I'm still not ready to talk about "he" or "she". I demonstrate "that" . . . I am pure *it* that was pulsing rhythmically.' Yes, Lispector's androgyny is the ideal. I mean, she's so femme, and so butch; she's butch *inasmuch* as she's femme. How couldn't you want that freedom? Likewise, in the club's dark box, somehow I realise my masculinity to its maximum extent – that which I am – through becoming-woman. And that's no paradox.

> Nothing is so ephemeral as a theatrical performance – it even differs from night to night – and, in an age when songs, concerts, films, books, the explosion of the Challenger, the inauguration of a president, can be reproduced over and over again, hoarded and stored, what Ludlam did on his little stage is remembered solely by people who happened to see him.

That's Andrew Holleran in his essay on Charles Ludlam's early 1970s Theatre of the Ridiculous. For me it just as well describes a night out at Cocktail d'Amore or Buttons.

Camp and wild, the Theatre of the Ridiculous arose in New York City in the same post-Stonewall moment as gave birth to our dance-music culture, which, prior to disco's mainstreaming, initially kicked off at places like the Loft and Gallery, and later at the Paradise Garage, with Black and Latino gay men at its core. At these parties, the line between gay and straight could blur. 'As David Rodriguez would say, "Straight to the next man!" or "He's bisexual: he likes men and boys!"' said Michael Gomes (as Tim Lawrence reports in his history of the NYC scene, *Love Saves the Day*). 'There were so many people who were just sexual. A lot of black men would have sex with other men but didn't consider it gay sex,' said Nicky Siano. 'It wasn't about gay or straight. It was about,

"Hey, let's party!".' Sexually we're actualised on a spectrum which, though it has gravitational poles of greater or lesser probability, is nonetheless as inexhaustible as timbre or colour. How liberating, then, to throw your shabby inherited hang-ups out the window – and how nerve-wracking, too.

On the dancefloor I gravitated towards queer people. They were more attractive and more interesting. In contrast to the straights – on autopilot in our breeding-based society – queer people, I thought, had had to work to become who they were, and I supposed that that was why on dancefloors they usually felt more open and respectful. Yes, in Berlin's clubs it was the homos who were hetero (i.e. multifarious) and the heteros who were homo (i.e. homogenous). That's why, as well as the intense music, and although truthfully I didn't know many people there, I felt at home at Cocktail: in blue fishnets or ludicrous epaulettes or whatever, I felt free; in this ludicrous *mise en scène* – this industrial ruin that worked the trap – I felt free. And at some point the strange thought dawned on me: *this is a fabrication to which you go to get a dose of reality.*

In the aforementioned essay on Charles Ludlam's Theatre of the Ridiculous, a heartfelt homage to drag and camp, Holleran writes:

> Ludlam was comprehensive – pure theater. Which we were starved for – driven to his little group by the staleness of Broadway, the fatuities of a mass-produced, television-dominated, film-and-book-soaked century

> that gave equal time to the fall of Beirut and the fire in Michael Jackson's hair started by a commercial for Pepsi Cola. Drowning in what Godard said the West had simply too much of – Culture; on the lam from history, novels, films, the *New York Review of Books* – and none of them any FUN!

All of which captures the ridiculous theatre of clubbing, Saturday night's essential oblivion – the oblivion of this club Griessmuehle, the homely oblivion that undercuts us all.

■

The dancefloor below is a far-off fug of darkness, a dingy aquatic pool. From a rickety platform above, we watch the bodies moving, only faintly visible through their dancing motion, a shoal of fish intermingling below the water's dank surface, the etiolated strings of a Giacometti canvas.

The music is slowed-down electronic crunk. Its *largo* effect is as if, after an ambitious bump of ketamine, reality had lost track of itself – had, in clumsy slow-motion, split from itself and were trying in vain to grasp and catch itself, as the costumed bodies below us enact a languorous pleasurable pantomime.

This is the Cosmic Hole. It's the second of Cocktail's three dancefloors, hidden away at the back of the factory building. Its vibe is spacier than the main room. Overhead, a solitary red lightbulb is set in the high wall, a distant red dot emitting terminal cosmic pulses, rendering everything red, rhythmic, as the industrial space stretches away into night-time black.

'It's like we're in a movie,' Indrani says.

She looks at me pensively. I finally found her here five minutes ago, leaning alone on the unsteady proscenium rail.

I don't know what to say. I remain silent.

Through the mist I'm watching the two men behind the decks, the tall, bearded Trent smoking a joint and the fresh-faced Dama spinning a record. The track's a slowed-down early eighties electro jam where, on every off-beat, the snare strikes in cavernous reverberation, slam . . . slam . . . slam . . . buildings exploding . . . towers tumbling. (Later I'll learn that Trent and Dama DJed back to back in the Cosmic Hole for twenty-four hours continuously, a legendary set.)

A straight couple in matching rhinestone policeman's hats, pink and blue, elbow past us, descending the stairs down into the Hole. I feel woozy, the combination of music and heat and lighting perfectly expressing, like a living canvas, that tension, impossible to quell, of being here, embodied within the interior of an old building that, so familiar from these parties, the Sunday mornings of my recent life, will imminently never again exist, its corridors and rooms and darknesses poised only for the ravenous void, a veritable world that will soon be nothing, less than nothing, giving all our actions here – this eye contact, that thought, that lapel – a sense of . . . not profundity, but rather the opposite . . . that vertiginous sense, as in Valéry's *cimitière marin*, of being more identical with themselves than ever before:

> I no longer have any importance. Now I'm the present itself. My personality is completely wedded to my presence, in perfect harmony with whatever may occur. Nothing more. No further depths. The infinite has been defined.

I remove my cheap white gloves. Against the darkness my hands, fingers extended, become flowers blossoming, petals unfurling.

'Let's go down,' I say. I take Indrani's hand and we descend the staircase.

On the basement dancefloor I glance back. Indrani smiles.

No need to explain yourself. She knows.

■

A tall man in leather and amulets, a Bronze Age warrior, is fanning Indrani's face, while at the edge of the dancefloor there's a man and woman making love. The heat down here is brutal. Being in a milieu, a hazy middle, through dance eventually leaves you unsure of where exactly you are: the distinction between outside and inside is collapsing in this soon-to-be-destroyed building.

'I feel like we are in a film in here,' I shout.

'You already said that, babe.'

Kraftwerk's 'The Model' comes on, slowed way down, and one or two people cheer (I hear myself among them), and Indrani moves her head to and fro. And Indrani's bindi resonates with the rhinestone police hats. And we entwine hands, then she lets go, and the electro emits spirals, and my ears become spirals, and the distant red bulb's dot stretches out into a line, and my eyes, following that line, become stretched in red lines, and my mouth becomes stretched into a red caricature of my mouth, and here in the middle of the dancefloor, the world stretches and is wildly exaggerated, more truly itself than it's ever been before. And on the ground before my harlequin striped socks, there's a furry hobby horse, mute and inexplicable. Intensely, the hobby horse regards me. And now, as in a painting, a burnished late Rembrandt, wherein the force of condensation and focus brings us back to the reality of, say, that pair of thick black shoes, paradoxically through making those black shoes vividly strange, or as in a poem, wherein the condensation of image and vortex of language, away from all utility, brings us back to the polymorphousness of language itself, so too now on this dancefloor the absurd parade of fashion and play and pantomime, set to synthetic electronic sounds, brings us back, through collective estrangement, to whatever it is that underlies our everyday reality and which is usually occluded. And as soon as I think this grandiose thought, I go to type it in my phone, to take a note, but my phone screen's a humid blur and after a few squint-eyed seconds I give up, and it doesn't take long for the night, too, to become a humid blur, a lurid smearing of pink into red, of blue into yellow, each colour intermixing to beget some new mulch, red and white making pink, and yellow and blue making green, and pink and green making blue, and so on, wonderfully dirty and wonderfully fecund, and wonderfully destructive, too, smearing Saturday night into Sunday morning till somehow Indrani and I, in the harsh drizzling daylight, are sitting on a bench beside the pink furry rocking horse, and of course Indrani, who enjoys herself till her body fails and we've collapsed together on this S-Bahn platform, collapsing a few metres from a bearded uniformed cop, who may or may not actually be a bearded uniformed cop, ultimately doesn't really care that much, since she and I are drawn to each other for who we are rather than who we're not.

Sister; Worm

SASKIA MCCRACKEN

'I have said to corruption, Thou art my father:
to the worm, Thou art my mother, and my sister.'
Job 17:14 (KJV)

'Stoop, selfish Pride! Survey thy kindred forms,
Thy brother Emmets, and thy sister Worms!'
Erasmus Darwin, The Temple of Nature, Or, The Origin of Society (1820)

Each week I go to the governor's house to unwrap and catalogue the parcels. It's June and the trains are empty, rattling quietly towards Hammersmith with the windows open, the itch of sweaty skin against the seats and the way there are more trees the closer I get to the prison. The arched entrance to HMP Wormwood Scrubs is flanked by red-brick columns with thick white keystones. I never go in. Instead, someone buzzes me into the building next door, more red brick, all grey corridors inside. There are parcels of every shape and size against the hallway walls. Square boxes, thin brown paper rectangles, thick white lumps in shapes without name, cardboard tubes. Some thrown together roughly with the edges torn; others taped and taped so tight it's hard to open them.

I go up the stairs to a room where a small radio plays 'Uptown Funk' all summer. The windows barely open and a small plastic fan creaks from side to side, blowing curls of torn-off Sellotape across the floor. Against every wall there are shelves filled with more packages. Some of the shelves display the items we've been sent, each with a paper tag tied to it with string. The tag is labelled with a number, category, title, place of origin and a coloured sticker: red, purple, orange. Prison, psychiatric ward or detention centre.

I put my bag down by my chair and unpack my lunch. There are bubbles on the inside of the plastic takeaway box and my water bottle is warm. I am not going to the hospital next door for lunch again, though. I go downstairs, put my lunch and water bottle in the fridge and go back up to the room. My ring binder is already on the trestle table, surrounded by boxes. I sit down and turn to where I left off yesterday, halfway down the page. The last item I catalogued was a bar of soap carved into the shape of a dove. It smelt like all unscented soap does – like school. The dove sat on the shelf with my label: the number, category – soap carving, untitled, HMP Shotts, red.

I take the first thing in front of me. It is small, square and flat. I tear off the tape and peel back the edges of the paper. Inside is a cheap canvas, face down. The artist has signed the back. They are not supposed to do that. I cover the signature in blank labels and turn it over. It is oil paint, deep dark blue all over with a few flecks of yellow in the middle – maybe a horizon, maybe not. There is a piece of handwritten paper giving the artist's details. All the pieces come with one of these. They don't have access to computers and printers. The handwriting is bad but more legible than most. It is called *Nocturne*. I fill out the details, also by hand, in the printed-off spreadsheet in my ring binder, for the data-entry team, which is one man downstairs who is tired most days. Then I write out the details on a tag, tie it to the painting and put the piece on the shelf next to the dove. I open the next parcel.

Halfway through the morning Natalie comes in and sits opposite me to catalogue more items. She is quiet and wears a red baseball cap indoors. The fan and the radio seem louder when she's there. Sometimes she taps her trainers to the music or comments on the heat and wafts her cataloguing pages like a fan against her neck. She's volunteering while on bail. It's the first time she's been able to use a phone in a while and she often disappears to take calls. Her son, she says apologetically whenever she comes back. I nod and say that I wish the windows could open wider and she agrees that it is very close in here. Occasionally I try to yank them up a bit higher, but the wood is bloated and rotting. Bits of peeling paint flake off as I pull. Outside, the columned gate casts a shadow across the concrete.

On my lunch break I sit on a plastic chair in the courtyard, which is bright with dandelions. Weeds are bursting from the asphalt. My pasta has congealed and is slick with a red, oily shimmer. I read that wormwood is a shrub that grows on wasteland and has healing properties. It is useful for treating parasitic worms. I am interested in worms because I am doing research on Darwin's last book, *The Formation of Vegetable Mould Through the Action of Worms* (1881). By day I catalogue, by night I shift around on my bed, trying to find a position where as little of my skin as possible touches the sheets. It is too hot to read, but I read. I read about Darwin, reclusive in his old age, writing letters from his home in the countryside to botanists and entomologists and farmers all over the country, asking them about earthworms. It is 1880 and he has realised that nothing – neither evolution or the people he met on his voyage around the world – fascinates him more than earthworms. What do they eat? Can they see, taste, hear, smell? Are they intelligent? He wants to know. He fills pots with soil and puts worms in them. Then he sits, waits, watches. I don't tell Natalie any of this. She doesn't ask me anything about myself. Besides, I feel self-conscious about it. It seems frivolous, here, to read about worms.

Back upstairs we continue working quietly while the radio plays and the fan creaks. There are thousands of submissions to this year's competition and sixty-three categories to place them in. There are delicate matchstick models and soap carvings, portraits and landscapes, poems, stories, textiles, sculpture, watercolours, pencil drawings, ceramics, woodwork, origami, collages. Sometimes we turn off the radio to listen to songs on CDs. Some of the artwork is light-hearted – there's a painting of a great white shark with a yellow and red packet of French fries sketched in its mouth, titled

Fish and Chips. Lots of the pieces are not what I expect to come from places like Wormwood Scrubs: portraits of smiling relatives from memory or photographs, landscapes of brightly coloured flowers and sunsets the artists could not have seen. But then I don't know what to expect. Something more painful, I suppose, like the entries in the writing category. The poets are playful or hide themselves behind rhymes, but the stories are naked. There are no characters. Only the raw feeling of missing everyone, each child's birthday, every tooth that went under the pillow. I never finish reading any of them.

At night I sink my teeth back into the soil. Over centuries, as they turn up the earth, earthworms gradually bury Roman bathhouses, drystone walls, ancient edifices. Darwin's farmers report the same process happening with stones in their fields. Each year a few more centimetres of each rock is claimed by the earth, as the topsoil rises and the stones are consumed. Vast human constructions are, Darwin writes, buried, concealed and undermined by worms, as they prepare the ground for all kind of seedlings by replenishing the surface of the muck. The act of breaking down organic matter, of composting, creates the potential for regeneration from decay. This slow, gentle destruction is full of possibility, potential. Monoliths do not collapse, but are quietly, incrementally sunk. I wake up in the pale dawn with the duvet on the floor, sweating, tasting mud.

■

One shelf is entirely taken up by a giant, wooden carving of a snail. A section of the shell is cut open so that you can see inside to a tiny box. Inside the box a tiny wooden man sits on a tiny wooden floor. There is nothing else in the box.

▪

We are preparing the governor's house for the judges to come and look at the work. We carry all the sculptures into one room, all the textiles into another, dedicate different walls to different painting categories and hang the canvases. Natalie is very short and has to stand on a chair to reach the top shelves as we move the artworks around. I say I'll do it, but she insists. I ask her how her son is. Oh, you know, she says, and shrugs, pulling her cap lower over her eyes.

There is one category that the judges will not come to inspect. Only one prison in Britain has facilities for publishing work in Braille. They sent us a handful of submissions on large squares of card with raised print. I run my fingers over writing I cannot read. Wow, I say, look at this. Natalie looks up from her phone and looks back again. One writer has shaped the raised points into characters from Pac-Man. Circles eating ghosts. I box them all up together and post them to the Royal National Institute for Blind People for adjudication. The rest of the judges in the other categories come to the governor's house and look at the pieces we have labelled, stacked on the shelves, hanging from every wall, and take notes. I wonder if the Pac-Man submission should be judged as visual work as well as Braille, but I suppose you can't enter the same piece in several categories or you'd have an unfair advantage. I ask Natalie what she thinks. She says she doesn't know but that her son likes video games.

■

Darwin feeds his earthworms bacon and cabbage to see which they prefer – bacon. He shines candlelight on them when they are making their burrows to see if their recoil – their usual response to light – is reflexive. But there is a delay because they are so focused on their work, because their attention is elsewhere. They must, he concludes, have a sort of mind that can be distracted from the external world of light and dark. Perhaps even a kind of intelligence. He plays them the bassoon to see if they like music. They cannot hear. This is a moment of epiphany for him. They cannot see or hear yet they have, he says – evident in their focus on building their burrows instead of acting instinctively – a kind of intelligence. He compares worms to an American intellect famous at the time, Laura Bridgman. She, too, was deaf and blind; she, too, was intelligent. His praise of invertebrate near-human intelligence brings the woman with disabilities to the level of the earthworm. As far as he is concerned this is a compliment to both her and the worms. Both have almost-human faculties.

Bridgman was the first deaf and blind woman to learn to communicate using finger spelling and writing after raised text was invented in the 1820s. She studied history, literature, mathematics and philosophy. Charles Dickens met her when she was twelve years old and wrote about her in his *American Notes for General Circulation* (1842), recalling her sparkling intelligence. That Darwin mentions her without explanation suggests that she was well known at the time. Her literacy levels, let alone her scholarly interests, combined with her blindness and deafness, were remarkable to her contemporaries.

The comparison between Bridgman and the worm does several things. Firstly, it denigrates Bridgman to the status of lowly creature, by virtue, it seems, of her faculties. That she was educated at a time when so few women were, and so was seen as a novelty, was no doubt significant as well. The comparison also elevates the intellect of the worm to near-human, or at least near-woman. Yet Darwin's analogy tells us more about him and his expected readership than it does about Bridgman. It doesn't tell us that she lost her hearing, sight, smell and taste to scarlet fever when she was two years old. Or that she developed her own language of gestures. Or what the New England Institution for the Education of the Blind was like and why she didn't eat. Or what she thought of the bust made in her likeness, which was taken on a tour of the United States to promote the school without her.

■

Instead of the empty, rattling train I take the tube to King's Cross. I am packed in with the damp shirts and loosening ties of the city and emerge into the bright light of heaving bodies rushing along the pavements. The institute is down a side street, where the roar becomes a hum. I step through the main entrance and feel the sudden chill of air conditioning on full blast. I'm directed to the lift and go up to an open-plan office. I'm introduced to the competition judge, who sits me down opposite his desk with a plastic cup of chilled water from the dispenser. He is wearing a magenta, silk shirt and has a grey ponytail and beard. He explains to me why he has chosen the winning piece from the selection of Braille entries. It is difficult, he says, to create footnotes in raised print – I'm not sure if he means in general or at the prison – because all the text is the same size. One entrant has created a system that involves having the footnotes as an accompanying text. He is excited about this. The Pac-Man is fun, he says, but this is exciting.

▪

We are all at computers downstairs, helping the data-entry man input all of our handwritten catalogue material into the online system. The winners have been announced. Besides individual prizes, there is a gold, silver and bronze award for overall excellence across all categories. The sculpture of the snail with the man inside is the winner of this year's competition. It will take centre stage in the brochure and gallery space. Some stories and poems are published in a pamphlet to accompany the exhibition, but not the ones I couldn't finish. After we have finished inputting the data, we need to pack the award-winning works for the gallery. Natalie and I go back upstairs with bubble wrap, brown paper and Sellotape.

We sit by the creaking fan and wrap parcels in every shape and size on the trestle table: square boxes, thin brown paper rectangles, thick white lumps in shapes without name, cardboard tubes.

■

Darwin does not mention Bridgman again in his book and dies soon after it is published. She is safe behind the walls of her educational institution and will not read his words. They will not be translated into Braille in her lifetime or in mine. She will not learn from him how surprising people find it that she can think. But she knows that already. She will not learn from him how worms have the power to bury as they regenerate the soil. She likes her institution. She cannot read and write anywhere else, cannot solve mathematical problems beyond these walls. But sometimes she wishes the monolith would sink into the mud. There are so many tourists.

■

I sit in the courtyard with my salad, leaves wilted, olives shimmering in beads, hunks of cheese with droplets on the surface. The sun burns the back of my neck and my hair clings to my skin. Natalie is on her phone, walking in circles by the wall where dandelions choke the cracks in every surface. Then she stops, throws back her head and laughs. She laughs and laughs. Eventually she hangs up, removes her cap and runs her hands through her hair. Her eyes are blue. She looks straight at me and smiles, then puts her cap back on and goes indoors.

■

I have finished reading Darwin and started writing. I am washing the mud from my tongue. The nights are getting cooler and soon we switch off the fan, close the windows of the governor's house, close our ring binders and leave for the last time. The gallery is cold. We wear jumpers indoors and blast the heating while we sit on the floor, surrounded by paper packages. The walls are ready for hanging. There are empty display cases everywhere. One of the gallery assistants comes through and starts filling them with labels. Once we've unpacked, we'll know where to put everything. As I open the first artwork, a vast cardboard box, Natalie disappears to take a call. Inside it is the snail sculpture. Pull away the edges of the box and place it carefully in the display case beneath, surrounded by small spotlights. I run my hand over the smooth, hard surface of the shell and look at the tiny man inside. Then I close the lid.

■

The year after I leave, the arts trust relocates to another building. The governor's house is not fit to use, is not fit for art – is undermined, I like to think, by worms.

Quartet

SONYA GILDEA

I

Even now, I am simultaneously travelling across this room and have already arrived. Reaching for the emergency cord, a low-hanging thread in half sway. It is thumb-shaped: a soft-ridged grip. I am on the turn. In movement, fluency.

There won't be another waking now. Not in memory, nor in time.

I am sweeping under her fall, her slow keeling forwardness. I am reaching to and for the right shoulder first, her chin is resting down. I am pulling her in. To what? To this? I am pulling her to me.

She is quickly young. She smiles.

She is broken. It is – and I know it, deeply, fully know it – over.

We are into this, a last part. And she – hanging now to my slow-folding body – knows it too.

We will relive this. She will be gone.
And I will, briefly, radiantly, remain.

A girl-child on ahead, distracted (no, absorbed), is called as though yanked gently (though wholly) back on a thread of narrow, startling light.

Whose is this light? Whose is the threading?

Navajo people refuse use of the person's name for at least one year after. *A tack of moons, I think, I hear . . .* Believing that to say the name – to have it worded on air – calls the travelling person back.

▪

This happening takes place in its own geography of time: a *sweetness* of displacement.
A bird flock thinning on the turn.

It is new currency to me, swift and entirely, fluently, paused. I understand it as though spoken. I understand in detail. It is temporary. I am glad of it.

And even now, in this remembering my resting heart rate slows. First, the left heart, then its kin.

Does the sway of this first scene have distinct light? A pre-light? It is memory-sweep. We are carried on an upswing while pressed, held (soft) to its undertow.

There is a wash over this image, over all that is seen; a grey, with a silver slick – a rinse, say. Grain in its saturation, and further back is iridescent with sparkle so small as to make you doubt it.

It does not change, not in any re-imagining.

> **Blackrock** | There, we'd seen the bay fill with tide, and empty out again. Night skies, when clear, gave the moon-quarter a start on that side of the four-storey building. The sick house.
>
> Her sleeping.
>
> A moon-cycle, I'd thought, I'd wondered. I may have whispered out loud.
>
> September, I had thought, without the word for it. The fifteenth, I'd thought, though unsure.
>
> – That was before.

Now | I am of this morning only. Leaving corridor, turning and taking the corner, arriving in. It is early, it is day.

There is a particular scent. Not only the scent of ending; its unique, distilled potency. But this other. It will outlast the room, and rooms, and corridors. It will outstay the building, the cold car and travel, the home-house. It will outlive the downstairs hallway, the air flights overland/sea and oceans. Again, outwith the Scottish house and hallway. It will remain. In my hair, hem of skirt, cuff of sleeve. It scents my skin, and I know.

So it does. Ten months, eleven months on.

This is Friday | I'd had things in my hands, both hands; practical, necessary of the minute things. Bags, three of them. And something under my arm? Another crossed-strapped over-the-shoulder zip bag and, on days wild with lack, something always (newspaper, magazines, post . . .) tucked under my chin.

One bag is fresh with clothes. Linen folded pleasingly on the seam, the crease. What is the ceaseless exhaustion to that one tiny image? Never was a fabric to hand during this time that could be felt for fabric only; always at skin remove. An absence. The self, elsewhere. Here, in fact, in this room, No. 34.

There is weight to these bags. Heft. Proper shopping. Bottled water. Sugar-free chewing gum. Price-tagged cardigan. Fresh cloves.

What is it, do you think, with the fresh cloves? And craving them? I make something up. But – they remind me of Donegal too, of her mother, of our home. The house by the river. Clove rocks, 1/4 lb, boiled sweets: glass jar – to metal scales – to trace-paper pocket. A tumble of sweets. Summer in the taste, after-taste. Laughing with July on your mouth.

I drink tea laced with cardamom, cinnamon, ginger. Some casting on ahead flavour that spices into these days with instant fleetingness.

Products. Her list. Essentials.
I save the note, a scrap of paper folded, refolded.
Breast pocketed.

- Maybelline eyebrow brush and dust pencil (double-ended).
- Yves Saint Laurent liquid liner, soft brown (without smudge pen).
- L'Oréal Age Perfect Serum. Pale Blue. Day and Night (without SPF).

Because, as Helen Mirren said – on the TV overhead – we are *still* worth it. We laugh. On that day, in that room, we both laugh. Weak from laughing, giddy, wry.

■

I think I am tired. Have I slept? I am without a tracking logic, without sequence.

There is no point at which these bags drop/fall to floor, no *gravity X time* to loosen them from my grip. My hands are instead (miraculously) empty. Without sound. There is only merging.

> DNR | What loan language did we use and not use to word this, she and I? . . . No one, I can recall no one, saying these words. A decision made in the negative. In the other. A consult in hand. A light held, turned. A formality. I know this. She knows this. We can rest down this small bird. Its feathery lungs drawing breath.

She smiles. We have made it so far. And I am here.

> That is, I am not variously; in the air, in traffic, in town, in A&E, in transit, in class, in line, in work, in absentia, in motion, in trouble.

So we can begin.

II

(**Bedside** | And here)

I am tucked the living length | Two hard-back chairs, their varnished (pine) armrests to my warm wrists. I lie the length, facing her. Positioned just so. So that hands, at untroubled stretch, meet and enfold halfway.

The window has been opened, and will now always open, to her left. And on her left, daylight will take her leave. That will be Sunday evening, tomorrow. 6:40 p.m. After teatime, I will think then.

This bed turned on its axis this morning, early. Wheels spun against carpet. Done, while there was no time to think other. Anna-Maria, manager, met my eyes just once, read like code, like rain.

In sync, we spin this bed out, into the unknown epicentre of the room.

Facing it what? – I want to say west. I say, west.

And in my mind this action repeats, in memory-loop. All motion, a sleeping-swerve, broad and slow, that continues, ongoing. Some airborne bent of will. Balletic.

Danny Boyle's dancing NHS beds opening the Olympics: a swirl of turning sleepers under a night sky as though synchronised swimmers.

An MGM musical in some underwater dreaming, where we – the faithful and spellbound audience overhead and above all – know like liquid, as shapes move into their intricacies of pattern.

An Irish child, I was one of the spellbound. Lone hours in the cold North Atlantic Sea on Maghera, practising for the call that would – that must surely – come from 1930s Hollywood. I was not easily discouraged by logic, nor linear time.

▪

It turns out, and I could not know this then, she will not, in any traditional imagining, move from herself upward. Nor away from, apart from, unpeeling, separate or ethereal. I do it with her. All but the last part. And I know.

All but the last part.

She will, instead, be sucked in slowest motion backward from this world. As though by thread, pulled in awayness. Until, bent forward and over at the waist, hands and damp hair flowing, she is reeled back in. Until I unrib her last hold finger by finger from mine.

I'm woken by a Sunday afternoon once. Early, late '80s? The wane of a decade that moved at the hips. She is thirty-one, thirty-two and has, by force of imagination, brought David G— choreographer of the National Ballet, into *Chandras*, a many-mirrored Cork City nightclub for rehearsal.

He will choreograph her girls under disco-lit glitter balls in endless, dizzying lightless day. *My baby moves at midnight . . . goes right until the dawn . . .*

They are many – twenty, perhaps thirty women, dazzling in joy, in movement. Dancers, yes, models, yes. Sandra, Casandra, Catherine, Tara, Fiona T., Fiona M., Lorraine, Anne, Trina, . . . They are a collective, her collective, and they are adored. *My woman takes me higher . . .*

They too lead from the hips. Step off from the left, already in motion, in charge. Mid-glide. *My woman keeps me warm . . .* They groove, drift about the disco floor in patterns that emerge and repeat in mirrored walls. Saturday Night Fever. They are on the beat, they are, sometimes, liquid. *You should be dancing, yeah.*

They could not be more alive. She could not be more alive.

There is no childminder, we are – as is often the case – right there. Sitting about in the raised, half-moon black leather disco booths. Little or no homework done. Watching.

All Sundays are some variation on this life-pulsing rehearsal. I am very young, but I know it matters. I can feel it. Not just in the dancing, but in the imagination of it.

And I know how it feels, because I feel it in my small child body; the bones in my feet; where my teeth rest in their resting bite; my ears – well, in this, I am used to music too loud to be safe.
But in all, I know she has marked it out as ours. Even though I am too young to know what that will come to mean.

The Savoy theatre glistens in darkness, tiered seating cascades down to an aproned stage and length of boardwalk runway. Disco lit for night. The place charged, loosely electric.

Whether you're a brother, whether you're a mother . . .

Music louder than all life. She is, just now, in her element.

■

But first | My ribcage pushes against the yet to come.
I snag air, slip-stitch it in and under for her. In and under. Hidden, certain.

It is a dense lateness. I take the passive weight of her open hand onto, and into, mine. Palm to palm in winter remembering.

> The winter of this remembering is a February one. My own. A cold first touch Infant early. And is to become a late wane moon at its outmost span and wing.

The hallway safety light| Its dim second floor corridor now a muddy, medical brown. I do not move. I will not move. I will move later.

We will do this for two nights.

My lungs, if I breathe well enough, can be hers. I suck her oxygen into the tiny lung pockets inside ıny own chest.

I feel air as it travels, spreads like mist, fills, releases. The small exchange in alveolar sac after alveolar sac. I feel, not imagine, my breath opening down in hers; patient, known air.

The lung-house of grief.

Grief, they say, going back to those who came before, in tracery and return, to wrench.

That which we are born to and with.

Her lung-house will fill. Not all at once, but steadily. Measuredly. I know this in forensic, lyrical detail. *A drowning in one's own lungs*. Though, I do not speak the words together in a group or patterning. Pleural space.

Now, a portal | our second to last. I know this too. I have not slept. I am wild with calm and knowing.

I take the full, softened weight of her left hand into and onto mine. A second remembering, she will carry no weight, only touch.

Walking fields on the easternmost edge of this Scotland, coastal paths that brink the North Sea, salted gusts rise out of oceans animated and in concert. Rarely quiet, rarely still. But, fierce. And perpetual.

This, a body of sea that reels out over the day, over the people, their thinking. Insisting on being central to it, not absolute, but within and unforgotten.

It is in and by these sea-moments my contract is made. A deal brokered in watery bent and knowing. Though, there is the imperative.

That imperative | is that I will go with her, as far as is imaginable. I will remain to the last, and then – *and this be the sovran piece* – if I can, I will continue on a fraction, a heartbeat or so, beyond the last. Just enough, to safety.

I will do it with her, for her. Except for the last part.

■

Now, this night | pushing out against it; steady in my rib work. There is a sound to this ceaseless pause, it remains a sound neither within hearing nor outside it. I record it on my phone in the half-dark. We have made ready. She is unravelled.

She has been younger than me my whole life.

Her hand is strong; veins working and bruised in colour against the hall nightlight, atop a fleece blanket, now a silver grey.

I will put this blanket into the hands of her youngest, her wildest. He, in turn, will pull the car into a motorway layby and sob into it. Howling. Unable to see. Unable to drive.
Not now, later.

III

Saturday night | her hand is raised, held in mine.

Eyes closed, she is smiling.
Saturday night.

Her youngest son, her electric charge, her house of laughter. He has – with the irreverence and joy of loss – put on music. This – he remembers too – is what matters.

You should be dancing, yeah . . .

Her hand – soft-wristed and weak in its slack – pumps in mine, in the music, to the beat, on the beat. She smiles.

Go out dancing.
If I teach you nothing else.

■

There is a certain spin, a turn about memory-use to this room and what is to come.

Teatime Sunday evening | People in houses and homes throughout the city finishing their tea. An Irish meal in the evening in place of dinner, which has been had (on a Sunday) at lunchtime. A gather in, a pull homeward, a returning. Tired children, end of day-ness, the soft tumble into a coming back. There is a Sunday evening scent. Specific. The tedium (maybe). A kind of treacherous boredom at having to (having to . . .) leave.

■

Exhausted by so much living, she sits back, fits against the shape of me. Her hair damp. The suck/release/suck of oxygenair. Rhythmic, restful – as though in and from the next room.

There is oil. Did I arrange such a thing, its ritual, its succour? I did, it seems.
Aged and fragrant.

In soothing low hum, unvoiced, distant.

> Myrrh, sweet cinnamon, cassia, olive oil. *And you shall make of these a sacred oil blended as by the perfumer.*

■

I am wide-awake tired, we are out on our last limb. We are alive to everything. The mind has all it needs.

I say I'll take it for her, instead of/as her, and do – our heads together. She is blessed in sound spoken, worded. She is, in some hearing, some interculture, absolved it is said.

Forgiven, I say, near her ear, skin close; *do you hear that, you are forgiven everything.*

There is no other quiet.

■

I open out the window. Press it from us. On the turn, I see and know. We have made it this far. How sweet are we.

I heel off my shoes, one and the other while still walking, already an end movement, a daughtering. I climb onto her bed, pulling her up and to me, wrapping around her shape.

We are ready. We are here. She will go. I will return.
But, only at the last.

She is, I can feel, pulling me with her, out to the slim edge. There is no language in this part, just its press.

Whatever it was that we had to do in this, we did it. It is the richest thing about us together. And, we were often lethal.

We don't need to understand now so much as know. She can go. And so, she does.

It is unlike flight; it is unlike anything living. There is no slackening, no lessening. There is a stop only.

I free my hand and move it down (down) to her wrist pulse.

You have done it, I tell her. You have gone.

The suck release/suck of oxygenair as though in and from the next room.

■

There is a brace of low light picking off each branch in the medicine garden. A sky burns.

A hand-written page from a noonday in the glasshouse and herb garden at Donnybrook Royal.

A posy of wild mint cupped in her hands.

It smelt of the wild mint by the river at the side of the house in Glenties, she said. Donegal, she said. Some great, reaching sorrow.

I am stunned she has ever been.

IV

And still I had not slept. Not since Friday, but the room that had been hers had to be emptied. An empty room, I had thought, but in a silence that had nothing else in it.

I drove there. I remember that now. I can travel this route in my mind; the lights, the junction, and the turn. Had I driven it sightless this next day? Unknown?

I cannot now remember the stairs, the lift, the carpet. That awful carpet, apologist carpet, a kind of surrender in it, a sigh toward what could be, but is not, home. Ill-judged.

I feel its surface sometimes, late at night, as though under my bare feet. I had never walked it barefoot, but the dry fibre, its weave, feels actual to me.

The next floor. Even now, arriving onto the second floor does not place itself. But the scent. I refuse the memory of this smell. It takes me at my knees, quick, slight – almost not at all – and brings some folding in and over, a midriff collapse.

The room. It is back-lit, lucid-clear and burning still. No. 34.
They'd closed the door. A kindness, a formality?
A little, perhaps, of both.

Angela, no Ciara, had the Hoover out, the flex curling the length of corridor. Sorry to be so inappropriately ongoing. They wanted to dispense their sorrow – but briefly, efficiently – and get on. It is the currency in which they trade. I knew this, and had – on quieter days – loved them for it. Loved their flock intuition to be thoroughly present in the doing of tasks that pull the rest of us only onward. Sequential, linear. No matter that the next thing be unremarkable. Better even that it be unremarkable.

It was her toothbrush that undid me. At the sink, unable to go on or go back. Held up against, and absent to, bathroom light. Bristles and dry paste. A tiny madness, a spark, a jolt of some partial, spatial lack.

I could not drop it into the bin. Could not make my fingers part to let go. So instead, I stood, unable. Instead, I packed it. Though for what? For when?

Sea-green bathroom tiles. I had thrown up that morning. Before leaving. I'd gone back into the house, up the stairs – some, two at a time – and threw up standing. Over and over, my body convulsing, one hand flat to the tiled wall, holding on, upright. Expelling sorrow, throwing it up, I thought.

Though, I also had not eaten, not that I can remember, not since Saturday. Couldn't. And the migraine made water impossible.

■

I would (have to) step across the door-sill of Room 34; its wood-coloured, wheel-marked veneer, and into the narrow shoulder-width of hallway. So as to stand, facing the blank quiet of window opposite.

I knew that this must happen. I had spoken it to my morning self, putting on socks, tying laces. Out loud. Wondering – stunned, light-headed – what it would be to do this.

In muscle memory, what I had already gathered into DNA is that I would have to – somehow – walk back out again. Out of the now emptied room and then, the building. Leaving in the continuous. I didn't know how. And didn't yet have the word for not knowing how.

> There's no waiting-station, no liminal drift, no sheltering lean-to where this onwardness might be paused. Where some folding back into this time continuum could begin.
>
> They (the people/company/organisation owned the room. It had to be emptied, paid for, and then, returned.

I have never dreamt of that room. It remains stopped in time, untouched, and empty still. I can imagine if I were to drive as

I must have done that morning, through gates, up the avenue and park in the bay opposite, I would find the room exactly as it most was. Not before – while she was still alive – nor after, having emptied it out. But no, the third one, wholly in its own imagination.

■

Now | on this fourth morning, I walk myself into the room because I must. The resistance becomes physical. I am sucked backward, slammed and bewildered against some further, unexpected, opposite wall. Wrenched from standing and nailed to standing both.

It was – I knew – ridiculous to have done this, to have come here the next day. The day after. To have brought myself here; to knowingly bring such a thing to its roofless apex, and just now. Foolish.

But with the speed accuracy that comes with outright sleeplessness, I had scanned what the options might have been. In real-life time. In world time. Each option, in their way, unthinkable.

We had howled laughing here. Became hysterical. Made plans. True plans. Notebooked them.

Two bottles of good perfume.
One, Dior and the other Chanel.
The Dior was, it turns out, for Room No. 34.

After I'd pulled myself back to upright and opened the wardrobe. After I'd pushed the windows open, out to the winter-flowering tree, white for late October. After I'd registered the morning light, low and winter sharp. After some air taste I would not taste again—

I sat on the edge of the bed, dropped sideways and laid my head down where hers had lain. Curled up and waited to know every atom of this room from precisely here. To see only as she had seen. The angle slant of how wall, and floor, and sky appear and rearrange desolate. The underside of a wooden bird box on that winter tree. The catch of web under second-floor eaves. (Eaves in sunlight she said she'd give anything to take a sweeping brush to.)

I can feel the bed to hip and bone. See for her, feel in her place, sleepy and waking. Her panic now begun, the tiny pre-drowning, her air already taking water.

My panic, lying there, stops to quiet.

■

I reverse, backwards, out of this empty room filling it with her perfume as I go. Slowly, arm raised, spraying onto the air: Dior, the Parisian scent. And close the door.

Coda

On the rise of Temple Hill, before cresting and then down into the city village, there is a large, neon sign. Two lanes empty of traffic amid new roadworks; a cycle path and bus lane to my driving left, when emerges a billboard-size VMS digital display.

A burnt orange digital text on black.

BUSINESS
AS USUAL

I smile. In preimage, wintered. A sister-Wednesday. *7 a.m. New Year's Morning*. Berlin, 1930 (*László Moholy-Nagy*). Also, dry and cold in silvers. A ground frost whiting out in shadow patterns. A night wind and road-sweepers clearing all. A city on waking.

From *The Ninety-Nine Names of Those I Love the Most: Four Dagli From Saudi Arabia*

TRANSLATED FROM THE FILIPINO BY ALTON MELVAR M. DAPANAS

Translator's note: Transplanting the báyot, translating the dagli

In some regions in contemporary southern Philippines, the báyot refers fluidly across the spectrum, from the effeminate gay (cisgender) man to the non-binary femme to the transgender woman. In certain contexts, it may even extend to cisgender women who 'act' camp or lean towards drag.

Historically 'male cross-dressers', according to the 2020 *Oxford Encyclopedia of Women in World History*, performed important ethnopolitical and socioreligious functions in precolonial times in some parts of a land mass which, based on ethnohistorian Oona Paredes's archival research in Spain, was called *las dychas islas* (literally, 'those said or aforementioned islands') along with the Marianas and, much later on, the Philippines, after Spaniard monarch King Felipe II. As a gender referent the báyot has long been documented, as early as 1680 CE in the fifty-five-volume *The Philippine Islands, 1493–1898* edited by Emma H. Blair and James A. Robertson. The báyot were demonized by Spanish friars in the latter's colonial quest of *reducción*, to further spread Christianity as mandated by Pope Alexander XVI's *Inter caetera*, or Papal Bull, of 1493. Since then, báyot has become a derogatory term, a curse word, for cowardice, frailty and weakness. (See, for example, the tirades of current Philippine president Rodrigo R. Duterte – known for his sexual assaults, doublespeak, misogyny, incompetence and extrajudicial killings – against his political rivals.)

In other ethnolinguistic groups in the southern Philippines, gendered identities which defy Western subjectivities may include the Tausug *bantut*, the Teduray *mentefuwaley* and the Sinama *dnda-dnda*. Among the counterparts across the globe are the Albanian *burrnesha*, the Brazilian *travesti*, the Chinese *yinyang ren*, the Ethiopian *ashtime*, the Indian *hijra*, the Indonesian *waria*, the Malagasy *sekrata*, the Malaysian *mak nyah*, the Maori *whakawahine*, the Mexican *muxhe*, the native North American *two spirit*, the Omani *xanith*, the Samoan *fa'afafine*, the Siberian *ergi*, the Thai *kathoey* and the Tongan *fakaleiti*.

■

Within the tradition of Philippine literature written in Filipino (an oeuvre independent from Philippine literature in English and literatures of other local languages), the dagli is a short prose piece which may either be flash fiction or flash non-fiction, or both, or neither.

The dagli is a genre that proliferated in vernacular magazines, newspapers and periodicals at the dawn of the twentieth century, after the Treaty of Paris, when the Americans took full control of the Philippines and the English language was imposed by the state. The 1994 *Encyclopedia of Philippine Art* defines the dagli loosely as 'vignettes or sketches' that could be traced back to the Tagalog *pasingaw*, the Cebuano *pinadalagan/binirisbiris* and the Spanish *instantanea/rafaga*, as 'short account[s] that assumed a number of function[s] ... [characterized by] spontaneous and hurried quality ... [either as] an explicit expression of a man's love for a particular woman, but at other times, it became highly polemical, expressing anti-American, anti-clerical themes.'

Growing up in the northernmost region of the southern Philippines, Stefani J. Alvarez's native tongue is Cebuano Binisaya, not the Tagalog-based Filipino she writes in. Subsequently, her writing is entangled with other motifs and topicalities outside of sociolinguistic concerns, such as her dagli's I-persona as a báyot, a migrant Filipino worker, a son and sibling, a transgender woman in a patriarchal and conservative country, a sex worker, etc. This linguistic and thematic multiplicity raised many aesthetic and textual challenges when translating her dagli, especially in terms of rendering her voice. The language, on the surface, is Tagalog, but the nuances, the embodied experiences, the structure and, as Alvarez has said in an interview, 'my soul', are all in our shared native tongue, the Binisaya.

As an emerging translator, I also considered my presence/ absence in the source text, bearing in mind the unique role of translation in giving wider platforms and postulating identities from the post/neo-colonies, thus contributing to and disseminating, in this context, Anglophone-generative literatures. One advantage here, however, is that Alvarez and I were born and raised in the same city and have the same native tongue, or at least the dialectical variant of the Cebuano language spoken in Northern Mindanao, more than a hundred nautical miles from the language's literary center, Cebu.

I write in English (and in Binisaya), while Alvarez writes in Filipino, 'a legislated and developing language, which is Tagalog-based and is taught in all the schools of the country, and of course reinforced by Manila-based mass media', according to the Boholano poet Marjorie Evasco. Our approach to and cognition in the language may be the same. It is in this sense that I would still like to be up front about my possible mistranslations as, borrowing the words of Filipino scholar Vicente L. Rafael, it 'is predicated on the inevitability of mistranslation . . . spawns undecidability, ambivalence and, at times, violent misinterpretations.' This was, admittedly, an aspect I kept coming back to and still constantly worry about.

These concerns, along with other acts of translation, required careful attention and a hint of experimentation, as I grappled between translating 'word for word' and 'sense for sense'. Stylistic questions emerged: how to translate the confessional style rhetorically enmeshed with Filipino gayspeak – locally, *swardspeak*

– and working-class sensibilities, which, in the original text, is already linguistically layered (as Filipino is Alvarez's second language)? In what ways might word order, brevity, and thematic progression shape the target text? What shifts in translation am I willing to alter from the source language to the target language? What boundaries will I have to redraw and revisit from time to time?

From here I began to see larger questions: how to translate a minority culture – which Alvarez and I both belong to, as queer Filipino southerners navigating the literary spaces of Manila, the country's cultural center, and the West – into a dominant world language without treating the work as some sort of postcolonial exotic which may, however, serve as its currency for publication? Given the subversive historical tradition of the dagli – a genre which defied the Euro-American short-story form and the English language during the American occupation in the Philippines and long after it – can the same genre and the act of translating it be exemplified as a contact zone between the colonizing genre and language to the colonized? Similarly, Bikolano fictionist Merlinda C. Bobis has asked, with multilingual communities like the Philippines in mind: 'But what if the different languages co-habit in one text? How can translation begin as a decolonial urge that facilitates an empathetic collaboration among differences, so they can resolve each other into meaning?'

Alvarez has produced a body of work that portrays longing, torment, defiance and trauma in pieces which convey, in the words of Ina R. Silverio, 'unflinching honesty and such poetic grace' and which are 'to the point, poignant and painful'. Alvarez's dagli is heavily informed not only by her material reality but also by the language and genre she is writing in. Her work can be understood (and best appreciated) in the larger geopolitical landscapes of diasporic/migrant writing, working-class literature and postcolonial/transnational queer theory.

■

David Lazar has written that 'genre and gender are indissolubly linked, etymologically intertwined'. Such a notion also brings to mind the similarities between transgender and 'transgenre', in the words of Kazim Ali, in *Bending Genre*. Similar resonances can again be seen in Barrie Jean Borich's essay 'The Craft of Writing Queer', where she draws out the parallels between the 'fluidity of gender' and the 'shifting genre parameters' which questions heteronormative storytelling and cisnormative stories, not only in terms of the subject but also in style and structure.

Gender and genre or 'gendered bodies' and 'genred writing', to borrow from Ali, are both social constructs.

Rahman

Para akong pusang gutom na sumalubong sa kanyang amo pagbukas ng pinto. Ngunit hindi ako ngumingiyaw sa gabing iyon. Humahagulhol. Nakaluhod. Nakakapit sa mga paa ng lalaking itinuturing kong panginoon sa loob ng tatlong taong pagiging OFW rito sa Saudi Arabia.

Marahang-marahang kinalas niya ang aking mga kamay. Maingat na maingat. Dahil tila nais bumaon ang aking mga kuko sa kanyang suot na puting thawb. Inangat niya ang aking mukha. Ni hindi na niya pinahiran ang aking luha. Ibinuka niya ang pagitan ng aking mga labi tulad ng pagbukas sa isang jewelry case. Nagpakilala ang espiritu ng rum and Coke sa aking bunganga bilang choice of poison sa nakaraang magdamag nang sumama ako sa isang bagong kakilalang Saudi.

'Abdulrahman . . . ' Parang sagradong surah nang bitawan ko ang kanyang pangalan.

'Astroglide.' Nag-anyong mabait na kaibigan. Kinilala niya ang isang bote ng personal lubricant sa tapat ng kama.

Ngayon, naramdaman ko ang kanyang kanang palad sa aking ulo, at dahan-dahang kinuyom ng kanyang mga daliri ang aking buhok. Napaigtad ako. Parang pusang ibinitin. Pinalagkit at pinadulas ang buo kong katawan ng aking sariling pawis.

'Where is your Mister Astroglide?' Sindiin ng pagkakabigkas niya nang pilit niyang ibaon ang bote sa aking likuran.

Wala akong ibang pangalang bibitiwan. 'Abdulrahman . . . ' pagmamakaawa ko.

Mas mahapdi ang sumunod na pagbaon. 'Is it more pleasurable than this?' Napapikit lang ako dahil totoong mas madulas ang lubricant kaysa idinura niyang laway sa aking mukha. 'Where is he?'

Nasisilip ko sa ilalim ng aking kama ang hinahanap niya, kasama ang aking alaga. Sa pagkakataong iyon, una kong narinig ang kakaibang pagngiyaw ni Sama. Tila isang munting halimaw na nais kumawala.

Rahman

Like a starving cat, I welcomed him upon arrival. But that night, I didn't yowl. I wailed. I bowed down. I clung onto the feet of the man who has held me in servitude as a migrant Filipino worker here in Saudi Arabia for three years.

He untied my hands eventually. Although very delicately. Because my nails seemed to yearn sinking against his white thawb. He hoisted my face. But he didn't dry my tears. Instead, he opened my mouth, agape, like a jewelry box. What made its way inside was his choice of poison, rum and Coke, when he knew that I hung out with another Arab man last night.

'Abdulrahman . . . ' I implored, breathing out his name like a sacred surah.[1]

'Astroglide.' Now wearing the facade of a good friend, he

1 The equivalent of a 'chapter' in the Quran.

uttered the label of the personal lubricant from across the bed.

His right palm against my head. His fingers gently brushing through my hair. My body twitched. Like a cat about to be hung. My sweat lubricating every inch of me.

'Where is your Mister Astroglide?' His voice just as brutal as his burying of the bottle in my behind.

There's no name to give. 'Abdulrahman . . . ' I begged.

The next thrust was even more gut-wrenching. 'Is it more pleasurable than this?'

I just closed my eyes because the lubricant was slicker than the saliva spat on my face. 'Where is he?'

I could see who he was looking for – from under my bed, with my pet. It was only then that I heard Sama's odd yowl, like a little monster wanting to break free.

Rahim

Para akong patay na fetus. Hubo't hubad na nakahiga sa sahig na marmol. Bangag ang pagkatao. Parang nilason ng sambanig na Cytotec.

Hinila niya ako sa banyo. At iginiya niya akong mahiga sa bath tub. Para akong nasa garapon na ibinababad sa formalin nang maramdaman ko ang pag-angat ng maligamgam na tubig mula sa gripo.

'I am sorry.' Ngayon lang siya nakapagsalita. 'I am Abdulrahim.' Ngayon lang siya nagpakilala.

Inangat ko ang aking mukha. 'It's okay.'

Nakatulungko siya sa pagkakaupo sa gilid ng tub. Ilang oras din siyang nakadapa kanina sa ilalim ng kama. Parang biktima sa gitna ng civil war sa Syria.

'What's your name?' Hindi ko siya nilingon upang ipahalatang di ako interesadong sagutin ang kanyang tanong. Sa halip, nagsindi ako ng yosi. At pinilit kong ngumiti.

Pinatay niya ang gripo nang mapansing aapaw na ang tubig sa tub.

'Thank you.' Nakatitig lang ako hanggang sa huling patak ng tubig sa tubo.

'As much as I want to help you but . . .' Inilapit niya ang ashtray nang mapansing nalalaglag ang abo mula sa dulo ng sigarilyo.

'Mafi mushkilah . . . ' Pinilit kong ngumiti uli. Simpilit ng pagsasalita ko ng Arabic na nangangahulugang 'walang problema' o mas ibig kong sabihing okay lang ako.

'He's your boss?' Nakatungo ang tingin sa humimlay na red Marlboro stick sa ashtray.

Dumakot ako ng tubig. Binasa ang sariling mukha, ang leeg, ang braso, ang balikat. Kung nadidilaan ko lang ang sariling balahibo tulad ni Sama, hindi ko na kailangan ng tubig upang hugasan ang sariling kahubdan, at kirot na nararamdaman.

Wala akong bibitiwang salita. Wala akong babanggiting pangalan. O kung sinuman man siya. O kung anuman ang naganap kanina. Umiling ako. Pumikit. Dahil ang lalaki kanina ay hindi ko lang boss. Ang lalaking iyon ay ang aking diyos.

Rahim

Like a dead fetus, I lie naked on the marble flooring. My entirety, drugged. As if overdosed with Cytotec.

He pulled me into the bathroom. And guided me to lie down in the tub. I felt like I was inside a jar of formaldehyde when the lukewarm water from the tap touched my skin.

'I am sorry.' Only now could he speak. 'I am Abdulrahim.' Only now did he introduce himself.

I tried to face him. 'It's OK.'

He was sitting on the side of the tub, hunched. The whole time earlier, he was under the bed. Like a victim in the middle of the Syrian civil war.

'What's your name?' I didn't look in his direction on purpose, as an indication that I wasn't going to answer his question. Instead, I lit a cigarette. And forced a smile.

He turned off the tap when he noticed that the water was about to overflow.

'Thank you.' I just stared blankly, until the last droplet fell from the pipe.

'As much as I want to help you, but . . . ' He placed the ashtray near me upon noticing that the ember was about to fall.

'Mafi mushkilah . . . ' I forced myself to smile again. I insisted on using my broken Arabic, a phrase which means 'no problem' when what I actually wanted to say was 'I'm OK'.

'He's your boss?' His gaze fixed on the dying red Marlboro stick in the ashtray.

I cupped some water with my palms. Moistened my face, neck, arm, shoulder. If I could lick my own fur like Sama, I wouldn't need water to rinse my nakedness and this feeling of torment.

I won't utter a word. I won't mention a name. Whoever he is. Whatever happened earlier. I shook my head. Closed my eyes. Because the man earlier was not just my boss. That man is my god.

Malik

At sino nga ba ako sa buhay niya?

'You are my moon,' nag-anyong makata siya. Cliché na ang linyang iyon. Ngunit paulit-ulit pa rin niyang deskripsyon sa akin. Siguro dahil umaatungal siyang parang aso sa gitna ng kalaliman ng gabi kapag nasisilip ang kabilugan ng buwan.

Sabi pa nga nila, iniluwal ni Venus ang mga babae, at sa Mars naman ang mga lalaki. At siguro nga pwedeng i-justify na mula naman sa Buwan ang mga báyot.

'How 'bout me?' balik-tanong niya sa akin sa tonong naghahangad.

'My Lord, my precious King!' Para akong alipin na idinampi ang palad sa kanlungan ng hari. At dahan-dahang ipinuntirya sa kanyang pundilyo.

Nagkamali ako. Hindi siya mula sa planetang Mars. Hindi lang siya ang itinuturing kong diyos. Hindi lang siya ang aking hari. Dahil nasasalat ko. Ay sintirik at sing-init ng Araw.

Malik

And who am I to him?

'You are my moon,' he said, channelling his inner poet. Clichéd line. But he was persistent with his description. Maybe it's because he barks like a dog in the deep of night upon seeing the full moon.

They even say that Venus gave birth to women, and Mars men. So maybe it can be justified that the báyot came from the Moon.

'How 'bout me?' he asked me in a tone that's hankering for an answer.

'My Lord, my precious King!' I am a slave with a palm on the king's lap, gently aiming for his crotch.

I was wrong. He isn't from planet Mars. He's not only my god. He's not only my king. Because I can stroke it. As straight up and as scorching hot as the midday sun.

Quddus

Kanina pa nagkubli ang araw. At nakabubulahaw sa pagtulog ang pag-alingawngaw ng adhan. Ang hudyat sa pagsisimula sa huling dasal sa araw na iyon, ang isha. At aasahan kong maririnig ang kanyang pagkatok sa pinto. Babangon ako't bubuksan ang shower.

Nang nakaraang linggo, nag-message siya sa akin. 'I am waiting my wife to sleep then I will visit you.' Ngayon, 'I am waiting isha will start then I will come to you.'

At humarap siya sa qibla. Hindi lang bilang palatandaan ngunit parang pagdambana sa mga alaala. Ang larawan ng moske sa Madinah na nakakakwadro sa aming ulunan ay animo'y lapida. Bilang rekuwerdo sa sisimulan naming ritwal at pagsa-salah sa iisang kama.

ikaw,
at ako
narito tayo.
bismillah.
hugasan natin ang ating mga kamay,
ang pagitan ng ating mga daliri
palasapin mo ako sa tubig mula sa iyong bibig
sasalubungin ko ang iyong kaluluwa
nang iluwal ito mula sa iyong hininga
hugasan natin ang ating mukha,
ang iyong magkabilang tainga
iangat mo ang iyong mga braso,
at yakapin mo ako
haplusin mo ang aking buhok
at luluhuran,
kakausapin ng aking dila ang iyong mga paa
la ilaha illalah, muhammadan rasulluhah.
pagkatapos, tatahimik ang shower
sintahimik ng paglamon ng dilim sa liwanag
haharap ka sa qibla,
at maglalayag tayo sa king size janna
allahu akbar.

Quddus

The sun has long been hidden from sight. And what roused me from sleep is the echo of the adhan. The signal to begin the isha, the last prayer of that day. And then, I'd expect to hear his knock on my door. I get up and turn on the shower.

He messaged me last week. 'I am waiting for my wife to sleep, then I will visit you.' Today, 'I am waiting isha will start then I will come to you.'

And so, he faced the qibla. Not just as a mark of his belief but also in reverence to memories. The portrait of the mosque in Madinah framed over our heads, looking like a gravestone. A reminder of what is about to begin: our ritual and salah in the same bed.

you,
and I
are here.
bismillah[2]
let us wash our hands,
in the space between our fingers
let me sip the water from your mouth
I will meet your soul
coming out of your breath
let us wash our faces,
both your ears
lift your arms,
and embrace me

caress my hair

my tongue will bend

and speak to your feet

la ilaha illalah, muhammadan rasulluhah.[3]

then the shower will be as quiet

as the darkness devours the light

you will face qibla,[4]

and we will sail through the king size janna[5]

allahu akbar.[6]

---

2 In the name of God.

3 The belief of Muslims that Allah is the only god and that Mohammed is His prophet.

4 The fixed direction towards the Ka'bah in the Grand Mosque in Makkah, Saudi Arabia, which all Muslims face when performing their prayers, wherever they are in the world.

5 Literally 'paradise garden', final abode of the righteous.

6 A common expression that means 'God is the greatest'.

Jeff Bezos Talks to God

ROISIN KIBERD

T+1 minute

Static shots of a rocket in a Texan desert. The broadcast is live, backgrounded by the gentle hum of engines.

Six bodies are huddled inside the capsule; three men, fifty-seven, fifty-three and eighteen, and an eighty-two-year-old woman. They crossed the bridge, rang a silver bell, strapped in, and endured the countdown. Now they will be blasted into the sky, so far as to glimpse a fleeting oblivion.

Regret and possibility collapse as they depart the earth. The flames press down, the rocket jolts, and it feels like they're soaring out of hell. News journalists and bystanders gather on tarmac some distance away. On YouTube, a commenter types 'With that ship design, Bezos seems like he is trying to compensate for something.'

Everything here he has paid for; the richest man on earth and, soon, somewhere off-earth, too, on the way to other planets.

He views space as a 'sacrifice zone' for industry; we'll exile our problems and salvage our planet, under his guidance, under his control. The whole world under him, in fact, because what is this if not an expression of the politics of speed, of momentum, of power, and of *looking down on things*?

T+2 minutes

It's a beautiful day in the solar system, not that day and night matter up there. Jeff Bezos blasts through the sky with his brother Mark and Oliver Daemon, the teenage son of a millionaire who paid for the ticket – a real-life Wonka child – and Wally Funk, a woman trained for space travel by NASA in the 1960s, only to be denied her chance, and granted it again, by Bezos and the spoils of gothic high tech.

The capsule carries with it talismanic cargo: canvas from the Wright brother's aircraft, a medallion made from a piece of the first hot-air balloon and a pair of goggles worn by Amelia Earhart, silver tape on the lenses to keep out the blinding light.

One year ago Bezos stepped down as CEO of Amazon in order to spend more time thinking about ways to colonise space. His voice is nasal and squeaky. His upper arms are disturbingly ripped. He is wearing a cowboy hat and boots, strapped into his seat, and that terrifying thing he committed to doing twenty years ago has finally come to pass.

Each spacecraft launch is a precise act of violence; the hand of a god pulling them through the atmosphere. The G-force is battering their bodies now, weighing on their chests, draining blood to their toes. He doesn't speak because the mic is live, and because he won't be heard over the wailing of engines. But Bezos opens his eyes wide, now, and wonders if death is something you feel as it happens to you.

T+3 minutes

Elevator pitch: an 'everything store'. A website that will gradually, systematically, remove the need to leave your house ever again. A website that will replace bookshops, electrical shops, greengrocers, postal services, TV channels, Hollywood studios, logistics networks, recommendations of books, films and music from friends, and the need to think for yourself while using the internet. A Nightmare Network; a corporation so vast and amorphous, so rapidly evolving and ferocious, so hideously precise, that it consumes every other idea in the world for the rest of our human destiny.

Amazon began with a drive to nowhere. Bezos, aged thirty, and his then-wife, MacKenzie, aged twenty-four, were in their second year of marriage. He quit his job at a New York hedge fund and they packed their belongings into vans (the drivers were given no specific location, except to set off across America). On the road Bezos typed up a business plan, bouncing ideas off MacKenzie in the driver's seat.

Originally the business was called 'Cadabra', but they concluded that it sounded too much like 'Cadaver' when spoken over the phone. They switched it to Amazon, a river multiple times the size of any other. They moved to Seattle and the company grew to fit its name; multinational, fast-moving, famous for recruiting the best, the most Spartan and fanatical, and refusing to offer them perks. Instead of PowerPoint, employees are made to compose six-page critical essays, narrativising the customer's journey. New recruits are posed difficult, occasionally unfeasible interview questions; 'Why are manhole covers round?', 'How many fax machines are in America?', 'If you had 5,623 participants in a tournament, how many games would need to be played to determine the winner?'

Those are for the office workers. At the warehouses, they're ID-ed and drug-tested and asked if they can lift fifty pounds. Then the real test; the timed bathroom breaks, the hazardous conditions, the body in competition with machines. Occasionally warehouse employees pass out or contract and spread coronavirus, or experience miscarriages, or fall victim to a rate of injury eighty per cent higher than those of Amazon's competitors. Some employees – quite a few, really – have died, at warehouses in America and Poland.

T+4 minutes

This is when they know they've left Earth alive; when they see its surface shimmering beneath them. This is when zero gravity kicks in and the booster – that vast, aluminium phallus – separates and falls to earth, leaving the capsule suspended between the Earth's atmosphere and outer space.

Escalation. The internet is full of Jeff Bezos quotes, misty-eyed memes made by fanboys, pictures of him on stages talking about relentlessness and growth. But he's also known for what employees call 'escalations'; emails containing only '?', indicating annoyance, boredom or disgust.

Amazon's stock fell by ninety per cent at the turn of the millennium, and rose by sixty per cent in 2012, the year of the Mayan apocalypse. The pandemic brought about its golden age; profits tripled and Bezos added $70 billion to his wealth. Amazon developed its own brand of ambient disaster capitalism, one where it is part of the disaster itself, selling overpriced masks and hand sanitiser, working to make sure you'll stay at home, streaming TV shows and ordering deliveries on Prime.

Over twenty-seven years, Amazon preceded, then exceeded Google, eBay, Facebook and Alibaba. Its symbol is an arrow shaped like a smile, pointing off-screen, into the unknown – towards something only Jeff Bezos himself can see, a joke only he is laughing at.

T+5 minutes

$15 dollars per hour paid to warehouse workers, walking 15 miles a day and working 10.5 hours on the graveyard shift 'Megacycle'. 1.3 million employees worldwide, 89 per cent of whom admit to feeling 'exploited'. 100,000 warehouse robots. 6,000 dogs brought to work at the Seattle office. 275,000 office employees worldwide, with roughly 5,000 in Dublin and Cork.

4,000 items sold per minute in the US. 49 cents of the US e-commerce dollar. $300 million users over five continents, delivering everywhere excluding Cuba, Sudan, Iran, Syria and North Korea. $5 million in lost sales, during a 45-minute blackout in 2013. 75,138,297 products for sale across the site (things you can't buy: full-size homes, cars, cigarettes, live animals, prescription glasses, lottery tickets, guns, gasoline, facial recognition software).

4.2 million books. 29 ratings of my own. #201 in the Media Studies chart. #280 in Engineer Biographies.

40% of the websites on the internet, currently being hosted on Amazon Web Services. 2,000 data points collected per order. 43 seconds of audio recorded each time an Alexa accidentally turns on. 200 million Ring doorbells sold in 2020, with 22,000 police requests made to access their recorded content the same year.

25 years of marriage, and a $38.3 billion divorce settlement, making MacKenzie the third-richest woman on Earth. $5.8 billion donated by MacKenzie, so far, to 670 charities.

$500 million spent on a new superyacht, plus $41 million on a private jet, and $100 million on a car collection.

A 60-foot-tall rocket, reaching 2,200 miles per hour and 351,210 feet (higher than that pretender, Richard Branson, who flew nine days earlier).

$1.7 trillion market value.

4 minutes of weightlessness, in which Bezos floats and tries to forget.

T+6 minutes

At times, over the years, Bezos's ambitions for Amazon became unsound and unintentionally Borgesian. One abandoned plan, titled 'the Alexandria Project', involved stocking two of every book ever printed, and storing them in a special distribution centre. Another, titled Project Fargo, involved obtaining one of every product ever manufactured, and storing those too (both ideas were quickly pushed back against by Amazon employees).

Apparently Steve Jobs loved music, especially Bob Dylan's – this is rumoured to have been a reason behind his relationship with Joan Baez in the early 1980s. Job's love of music pushed him to launch the iPod and iTunes, and Bezos's love of reading did the same for Amazon and Kindle. Each figure was apparently driven to kill the thing he loved, or at least make life a lot more difficult for the people who create it.

In its early days Amazon held meetings in a local branch of Barnes and Noble, something Bezos has joked about in public speeches. He worked out early on that bookshops couldn't stock all the books in circulation, but that an online retailer could. He once told his senior vice president, Steve Kessel, 'Your job is to kill your own business ... I want you to proceed as if your goal is to put everyone selling physical books out of the job.'

T+7 minutes

As a writer, how can I tolerate Amazon and the existence of Jeff Bezos? How can I write about, and humanise, the man who has held my industry to ransom? Why do I sometimes use his website to buy ebooks and electric toothbrushes, notebooks and Bluetooth speakers, like so many of the other Bezos-hating writers I know?

I think Bezos understood, very quickly, that as humans we can tolerate an ambient sense of guilt – that it, in fact, plays upon our grievances and confusion, our way of understanding the world – and that this can be drowned out, temporarily, at least, through the instant gratification of online retail.

What Amazon gave us was convenience, and a bewildering range of ways to spend money, ordered and recommended to us by algorithms. What it gave us was the ability to rank and review, to make judgements, and to see ourselves rated in turn. Amazon played on our fear of becoming invisible. Like any all-conquering regime, or dictator, it promised us status in return for capitulation. At first it allowed us to review authors. Then it allowed us to review everything.

Don't we all, guiltily, enjoy this process? We all want answers. We all want proof that we are going somewhere, that it's *for* something, in this lonely, precarious life. We are all on our private journeys to the edge of the atmosphere, and we are all spinning out. Some of us will break through and reach other planets. Some of us will fall, in flames, into the sea.

T+8 minutes

He used to have problems with 'women flow'. In a 1999 interview with *Wired*, he explained his exacting, oddly revealing criteria for dates: 'I wanted a woman who could get me out of a Third World prison.' It never came to that; he and MacKenzie had twenty-four years of apparently harmonious marriage, then divorced in a frenzy of tabloid stories about dick pics sent to another woman, and a rumoured phone hack by the Crown Prince of Saudi Arabia.

One year later, he watched as she gave away settlement money and married a school teacher.

He never knew his father. He tries not to permit himself regret.

Now Wally is shouting, 'I love it! I love it!' They're weightless, which means they've stopped moving, and are falling. He watches his brother turn upside down, throwing Skittles across the cabin, and floating them into the teenage boy's mouth.

T+9 minutes

Here on Earth, we are entering the Twilight of the Dads; the *Dadderdammerung*; the years in which the most powerful, most visible, most wealthy men on Earth devote their time to defying time itself. The period in which a kind of prosthetic machismo, attained with testosterone injections and personal trainers and meat diets and, some believe, adrenochrome, becomes the primary engine behind historical events. We have entered the era of ultra-high-net-worth individuals, of glaring monopolies, of AI, the most invasive, self-fulfilling form of capitalism, and of technological life-extension.

He is its keeper, its exemplar, and yet he can barely understand it himself. He's tried; in 1999, using a short-lived Amazon Auctions site, he bought the skeleton of an Ice Age cave bear for $40,000 (a species known among palaeontologists for frequently breaking its penis bone in fights with other male bears). It didn't really deliver any sense of historical profundity. Then he bought the Clock of the Long Now, built to tick once annually, for 10,000 years. Its goal is to conjure a sense of deep time – perhaps it does, but Bezos remains a creature of the present.

This is what happens when infinity is your business plan. Every book, every object, every server hissing in a darkened room. Every minute – no downtime, ever. Forever in 'growth mode', a warehouse on every planet.

Now he confronts Earth's surface and wonders who is looking up at him, and who among them cares, and who among them is wondering and waiting for him to die. It occurs to Jeff Bezos, now, that this might be a good time to talk to god.

T+10 minutes

'Hello?'

'. . .'

'Are you there? I don't know if I believe in you.'

Silence. Then he notices that the others in the capsule are frozen in mid-air. Wally is smiling. His brother is floating, eyes wide, at the window. A red Skittle hovers near the Dutch boy's mouth (*What is he doing here? Will this experience change him?*). Through the windows the view is split fifty-fifty, between opaque white clouds and the darkness of space.

'God, speak to me. What is this?'

A thundering sound in his skull. A voice answers.

'Why are manhole covers round?'

'So that they won't fall into the hole!'

The voice grows louder, deafening, like a hundred drone metal guitars. 'How many fax machines are in America?'

The others still haven't moved.

'I . . .'

He has to admit that he doesn't know. Then he remembers that nobody knows – only god, really – and that the purpose of this question is to demonstrate the candidate's thought processes.

'Why are you asking me these things?'

'We have five more rounds to go, you know. This is only the screening call.'

'You think this is a joke? I funded a space programme to get here.'

'It's not really space, though,' says god. 'You're only just past the Kármán line.'

'That's technically space.'

'Sure, whatever. If you had 7.9 billion participants on a planet, how many games would need to be played to determine the winner?'

‘I don’t really know what you’re looking for here.’

‘?’

‘Please.’

‘?’

Then an explosion between his ears. Something shifts, and he allows himself to feel everything he has not felt for a very long time: confusion, loneliness, loss. Loss above all, because he has lost the world. Then they’re moving again, falling, strapped in for landing. The parachutes are out, and it’s over.

T+11 minutes

They exit the capsule, meeting cameras and family members. At the press conference, Bezos stresses that the flight was not meant as an escape: ‘The whole point is that this is the only good planet in the solar system.’ He thanks every Amazon employee and every Amazon customer, perhaps sincerely, perhaps as an act of implication.

Then he carries on as before. He tries not to think about the darkness he saw. He tries not to think, ever again, about the possibility of another Earth.

These Mutilated Angels

LYDIA HOUNAT

In the four a.m. spit of Cornish drizzle, trees turned to black deformities. I hallucinated their chatter as they whomped into each other, half-fighting, half-fucking. The dark sky was threatening and wobbling above the earth. Houses clung to the ground, windows ogled at one another, giant street lamps cast their cold light down, judging. The rain silently misted the village. I remember the attire of that night clearly, emblematic of the phase I was in: faux fur black coat, red velvet wide-leg trousers, platform boots, black crop top. The gazing headlights of cars intermittently passed by; stony-faced, locomotive monuments wheeling through the lanes. It was as though nobody was driving them but themselves.

There I was, a smudge waddling in the wet, losing my grip.

■

Burial came to me as a recommendation when I was seventeen. My writing mentor sat opposite me at a Caffé Nero in Piccadilly Gardens. After exchanging small talk, we began to discuss where I was at in my writing – nowhere. It would have been nowhere at the time. I opened up the notes app on my phone and handed the latest two or three pieces of spoken word I had threaded together for him to read. Memory fails me on what they were, except I know they must have been empty and lacking. My mentor eclipsed the studious silence, looking up at me, squinting his eyes: 'Have you listened to any Burial at all?'

■

Seventeen is a tender age – you want to say you have read everything, heard everything, seen everything. You nod your head, silently feigning that you have understood that niche reference, that quote, that joke. At least, that's how I was.

For once, I actually said 'No.'

He tossed his headphones to me. The track playing was 'Spaceape', featuring the Spaceape, from Burial's debut album. 'This is what you should be doing,' he said. 'You should be pinning sounds to these poems, street sounds. Have you looked at what Andy Owen Cook's doing? He's making these stories, Tales for the Night Bus. He's got Burial in the soundtrack – I'll send you the link.'

If I take myself into the window of that moment, Piccadilly Gardens dissolved. I surrendered to the Spaceape gliding and hopping over the throb and snare of Burial's drumming, the woah-wah . . . woah-wah . . . woah-wah, the jab of strings swiping the bassline, as the deep belly of the Spaceape's Jamaican voice rolled: 'creatures covered, smothered in writhin' tentacles . . . Stimulatin' the audio nerve directly . . . You wan' come flex with meh?' The melody embodied the speed of the underground, that visual vertigo where the eyes rapidly dart from side to side, as the carriage skates from the station into the darkness. That, interspersed with repulsive, slinky, sexual poetry – texture on texture; the faint aroma of old sticky spirits, oil spills glugging with the lingering rubbish smells of Dalston Market in the dead of night, in a tunnel, out of a tunnel, the gaunt face and dark circles of tired eyes. It was a pungent symphony.

▪

I meditated on that song awhile, then put Burial away for years. I'd heard him in the wrong place, the wrong time; it was sore, heavy on my ears, inaccessible.

Until, and memory fails me once more as to how or why, he returned to me when one day I found the LP, *Kindred* (2012).

▪

'Ashtray Wasp' is the third track on Kindred. It opens with the sound of muffled, siren-like pulses, which gradually build to a crescendo, the creaking of crickets, soft breath and whispers fading and emerging. There is a faint rumble of an underground train passing by, before everything dissolves into an echo.

Then, a rhythmic trudge of bass and snare eclipses the brief silence, slipping us into the first volume from a trilogy of melodies. The emotional, melancholic refrain that howls from the first minute in, a warped sample from Monica's 'Like This and Like That' featuring Mr Malik – her voice rendered almost masculine: '*I want you . . . I belong . . . to, you . . . now! . . . I used to belong . . . to, you.*'

This breathy 'to you' heaves through; sweeping across the regimented drumming and measured ringing.

▪

It was broken-hearted. It was the anthem of my second year at university, lost to bad boys, psychedelics and, in the background, Brexit.

▪

Burial remained anonymous for a time. In interviews (of which they had only given few), they reiterated that their anonymity preserved the sanctity of what all of this was about: the music. Anonymity posed the kinds of speculation that must have frustrated and humbled Burial, with theories that they were possibly another alter-ego of Aphex Twin or Fatboy Slim. In 2008, Burial left a note on their MySpace account: 'i wanted to be unknown because i just want it to be all about the tunes . . . my names will bevan, im from south london, im keeping my head down and just going to finish my next album […] i'll try put up a tune later'.

Even now, that is more than anyone would ever need to know directly from Burial. If you want to *know* who Burial is, you only have to listen to tracks like 'Ashtray Wasp'.

▪

Around the age of nineteen, I experimented heavily with LSD. I was looking for a connection to everything. A connection to myself. A connection I had thought was missing from me. And a reason to be able to resonate with the psychedelic cognoscenti I was reading at the time, Timothy Leary, Alan Watts, Ram Dass – to be able to say 'Yes, I also know what LSD feels like!' I thought that if I could see the real beauty hiding underneath the mundanity, I might be happy. I lusted for the glow at the end of trips, flaring up the world's halo. It would reveal the iridescent sheen across night skies, the flickering stars rendering you quiet and unimportant, as you melted with the rain, which in turn melted with the concrete. Thoughts would stagger, distracted by tumbling observations, the hypnotic glow of a petrol station at night, the blur of footsteps, as my words and giggles slurred together. The dry mouth welding the tongue and teeth stuck, as the mind sits paralysed; an onslaught of rainbow-coloured revelations unearthing the metaphor behind why you chose to wear this particular pair of shoes.

Acid, emotional and unpredictable, wants you to be aware of your own skin, your own thoughts. And I was abusing it on nights with strangers – cutting tabs into quarters and doling them out to mothers and their graduate sons. Longing for belonging. And how much I wanted to belong to the man I thought I loved.

▪

I want you . . . I belong, to you . . . Now! . . . I used to belong, to, you . . .

▪

02:17: a momentary breakdown where organ-like arrangements pulse, bar by bar, down down down, up up up, intermittent vocals staple the rhythm, which are then sliced by the continuous drum and whomp – the first buzz of a wasp-like groan emerges at 03:10. Angry, frustrated, the vocals wince and blur, the bass puffing. At 03:11, the second frame hustles and fuzzes into play.

▪

The stick of a night out glistened across my face, smacked with liquor and runny mascara, cigarette ash pinning my hair. Walking alone, the trees were animated and watchful, like playtime could end abruptly at any moment and night would collapse on my shoulders. Fatigue began to flood my body; my eyes were twitching, drooping shut. Perturbed mandalas furiously morphed inwards and inwards. A homely thought sliced the hypnagogia – coming home, slurping hot tea, warming my bones.

■

In 2007, Dan Hancox interviewed Burial for the *Guardian*. When describing his music, Burial visualised: 'I want it to be like a little sanctuary. It's like that twenty-four-hour stand selling tea on a rainy night, glowing in the dark. It's pretty simple.' They were sitting in a café, somewhere in south-east London, the home of Burial, the place which moves him enough to encapsulate its cadence in rainy soundscapes illustrated by various samples: vinyl crackle, video games, '90s RnB, acoustic covers of pop songs – the kind of covers you find on late-night YouTube trawls.

Though I first heard Burial in the daytime of Manchester city centre, that introduction forged an instant association with the night. I never forgot how quickly Burial connects to place, and how place is the currency of the music he creates. This connection compounds the feeling that that place conjures in you, which is the beating heart of what Burial is trying to translate – the reason why you are walking home with him.

■

Cornish 'mizzle', as it is known in the south-west, is an amalgamation of mist and drizzle. On psychedelics, it becomes a captivating phenomenon – it has a fairy-dust quality to it that catches the light in off-yellow street lamps and car headlights, shimmering the concrete, tacking the roads with sweat. The body is glittered with it. And the hair seems to separate into individual, damp electric wires, a hectic frizz. It gives the impression that you have just left the gym, or a nightclub. It was July, and the mizzle gently lathered my face in its warmth. Tiny droplets dotted my faux fur coat, my lashes and brows, the velvet on my joggers. They gently shook to the warble of 'Ashtray Wasp'. My headphones were shaped like soup bowls, steaming my eardrums as I trudged the winding road in Penryn, my head writhing with the sounds, my footsteps quickening in pace to match the throb and glob of the penultimate sequence.

▪

06:39: the melody softens, as if it were contemplating. The droplets on my skin and clothes quivered as I came to a stop in the road. The mizzle seemed to merge in movement with 'Ashtray Wasp', performing together. The sound of thundery crackle, a tiny sample from a cut-scene in the videogame *Dark Souls*. Hushed lyrics, the distorted remnants of vocals subsiding at 06:13. These sounds unthread quietly in a gasp, before halting completely in a brief, silent second. At 06:15, just halfway through, the sound of a train chugging followed by rain crackle leads for twenty-one seconds before closing up. The section is interrupted by a sample from the first second of Hiroshi Watanabe's 'Hikari', before giving way to the dying breath of Monica's voice, 'youuu . . .'. All this is pinned by a sound reminiscent of jangling keys, fading at 07:25. Only the falling crackle remains, as if lubricating the next verse.

As I looked, the trees were quietly conversing.

■

And then on. The boots of thudding bass rally the tune back, defiant. It peels away from contemplation and gets up at 07:32.

■

Burial is solitude. Burial is the long walk home, the retrospective state, mulling over details from the night, your ears ringing from loud music, your senses dulled but awake enough to remain watchful of fellow passers-by on their night pilgrimages.

This kind of music is not meant for scaling sweat-covered walls and strobe lights. The roll of melodies conjures lateness, outsideness, leaving. He says: 'It's more about when you come back from being out somewhere; in a minicab or a night bus . . . you've still got the music kind of echoing in you, in your bloodstream, but with real life trying to get in the way.'

■

I was on the way back from a lock-in at Falmouth. The evening had been an uncomfortable one, surrounded by people I did not know, drunkenly stepping into each other, tripping over chairs, weepy conversations over failed relationships. I carried LSD in a film canister everywhere I went, looking for an excuse to escape.

The little tabs glowed at the bottom of the dark cavern, stinking of plastic and developer. Each of them was stamped with the Hot Lips logo, their red tongues lolling and licking each other. My jacket carried the stench of beer; several pints wasted, drying stale into the hardening faux fur. Alienated by the company around me, depressed by the mundanity of alcohol's effect, I quietly went to the bathroom. On my watch, the hour struck eleven. I shrugged my shoulders, took the colour in my hand, and ate up.

Regret rose to my neck instantly. A flippant decision. Saddled with the guilt, things inevitably turned anxious within half an hour. My ears were fizzing from the cacophony of raucous laughter, spirits swilling from bottlenecks, swigs of ale and lager. A person across from our table was tearing up a beer mat, pulling apart its fibres, reducing it to tiny pieces which they dropped like blotters to liquefy in puddles of beer and tonic. The sensation of watching this grew nauseating; my eyeballs flipped inside my skull; how everything felt dry and coarse – the air had been sucked dry out of the bar; every edge seemed sharper, crisper, as though someone had turned up the room's definition. I dragged me and my come-up away from the table of people, and sat alone in a corner. I remained in a trance for however long it was. At three a.m., I stumbled out of the bar and into the isolation of the streets.

The only person I knew who would be awake would be my friend Jamie. At the side of the road, I texted: 'I'm on acid. Do you reckon I'm the substance and the drug is taking me?'. A whale of a thought at the time. But in that moment, it really had taken me. The road seemed to be whispering something unintelligible and I began to remember things that I wanted to forget.

■

09:22: the final sequence of 'Ashtray Wasp' emerges; choppy high-pitched vocals from Sara Bareilles's 'Love Song', covered by YouTube singer Jennifer Chung. They stutter and undulate down a scale, and something about the night sky seemed to glitch with colours matching the flutter of Chung's voice. It spurted navy, then light grey, black, then a bruised purple – in that order. It was as though the notes could penetrate the dense clouds, instructing them to change hue.

■

Deducing samples from Burial's discography is an art, and a quest that flummoxes his listeners. There are hundreds of online forums dedicated to unearthing a track's origins: that bar at the beginning; that brief crescendo at 10:00; was that drum used in an earlier album? Did Burial brush his shirt against the mic there, or is it Hope Sandoval's warped sigh? This guessing game, while adding to Burial's allure and elusiveness, builds on frustration – the minute you think you know what you're hearing, where you stand with him, he slips away again.

I hear samples from 'Four Walls' in 'Ashtray Wasp', a sensual breath flushing the face. At 10:19, a different breath seems to loop on itself, as if resigning. It contrasts the track's earlier aggressive jab and fizz; the unintelligible lyrics stuttering, pinned by hollow bangs of percussive beat – a harmony, but gagging.

■

I did not miss K. – I confess I did not really love him. It was he who seemed to margin the pages of my acid experiences; saving me from bad trips, making them worse, lacing them with laughter, then feeling left with a niggling discomfort. It seemed back then I was only interested in people not interested in me, yet somehow, we were living together, as I was made homeless after hosting a party that got out of hand. Sure, everything had been fixed by my housemate's boyfriend and the landlord never found out about the damage, but that was not enough to save me from the blame later on. I took it, and moved in with K. at his gesture, which I was very glad of – indebted, actually – but it complicated the relationship. He had been with other people concurrently and I knew I was a stop-gap – he settled for me when the girl he originally liked left him for someone else. That kind of situation amplifies insecurity – playing on your biggest vulnerabilities – but K. was not at the apartment that night. He was away, which meant I could go back and lose my mind in peace.

■

Mark Fisher notes the pain in Burial's music, describing the people on the album as if 'wounded or mutilated angels'. When asked if the pain is personal, Burial briefly pauses. It feels as if he is discomforted at this point in the interview.

'Yeah, maybe.'

▪

Burial quickly segues into Sam Cooke and creating hope in introspective, despondent music. He would rather find the antidote in creating tunes that resonate with the grief of his listeners, angel-people with broken wings. Burial's music is not an ode to 'counting your blessings'; it is more a room to take solace.

▪

If Burial's records are a medium in which pain is transferred, released and heard, then this essay may seem harmonious in that respect. Rather than hide the pain I was in, it appeared that Burial released the valve – I felt everything. Songs like 'Ashtray Wasp' narrated the rejection, the grief and contemplation of losing myself in an unnatural way. Something about the disfigured vocals of these mutilated angels tapped into the hard lesson I had been ignoring, that no amount of beautification in my surroundings, synthetic or natural, could heal me here. Psychedelics were my means of trying to reconnect to a world I felt was often ugly. I substituted their colours and melting fractals for an identity, that, owing to my mixture as a British-Algerian girl, I had felt incapable of having. I was unable to reconcile these two seemingly separate spheres of culture and belief; compounded by rejection and grief I lacked the language or awareness at the time to fully articulate. Perhaps that night revealed the connection in me all along, in Burial, in LSD, and that long walk home.

■

Rasheem Avalanche's cover of Brandy's 'When You Touch Me' twists and glitches down the scale, the notes drip and drip, as the steady vinyl-rain blurs with the final sample.

The sequence from *Dark Souls* returns: a Boss Fight cut-scene with Seath the Scaleless. The sound of crystals cascade and overlap, idiophonic triangles like wind chimes circle and spill. It's as though something is arriving, but the sound gives nothing away.

And with that, 'Ashtray Wasp' ends at 11:44.

Notes on contributors

Niamh Campbell's debut novel, *This Happy*, was published in 2020. She is this year's winner of the Rooney Prize for Irish Literature. Her second novel, *We Were Young*, is forthcoming with Weidenfeld and Nicolson in February 2022.

Brenda Romero is a writer and game designer based in Galway. Her work experiments with the intersection of game form and narrative prose. She holds a MA in Creative Writing and is now enrolled in Trinity College Dublin in the PhD English programme.

Claire-Louise Bennett is the author of *Pond*, *Fish Out of Water*, and *Checkout 19*.

Jennifer Hodgson is a writer, critic and editor. She is currently working on a book about the life of Ann Quin.

Nidhi Zak/Aria Eipe is founder of the Play It Forward Fellowships, poetry editor at Skein Press and Fallow Media, and contributing editor with the *Stinging Fly*. *Auguries of a Minor God*, her first poetry collection, was published with Faber and Faber in 2021.

Formerly an academic philosopher, **Steven Methven** now lives in Leipzig, where he writes and edits things.

Brecken Hancock's work has appeared in *Hazlitt*, *Best American Experimental Writing* and *Best Canadian Poetry*. Her first book, *Broom Broom* (Coach House, 2014), won the Trillium Book Award for Poetry.

Liam Cagney's music writing has appeared in *The Irish Times*, the *Guardian* and *The Spectator*. He was shortlisted for the White Review Short Story Prize, and he is currently finishing a book on Berlin club culture.

Saskia McCracken's (she/her) publications include *Imperative Utopia* and *Zero Hours*. Her work has appeared in *Magma*, *Datableed*, *Amberflora* and

Zarf, and has been anthologised by Dostoyevsky Wannabe, Essence Press and Spam Press.

Sonya Gildea is selected for Poetry Ireland Introductions 2021–22, a recipient of an Arts Council Literature Bursary Award and winner of the John McGahern Award (2021). Her work is published in the *Stinging Fly*; *Crannóg*, *The Irish Times*; *Hold Open the Door* (UCD Press 2020), and elsewhere.

Stefani J. Alvarez (she/her) is a transgender Filipino woman, born in Metro Cagayan de Oro in the southern Philippines. She is the author of *Ang Autobiografia ng Ibang Lady Gaga*, *Kagay-an*, *At Isang Pag-Ibig sa Panahon ng All-Out War* and *Lama Sabactani: Isang Nobela*.

Alton Melvar M. Dapanas (they/them) is author of *Towards a Theory on City Boys: Prose Poems* (Newcomer Press, 2021). They've been anthologised in *The Sun Isn't Out Long Enough*, *Now I Know*, *Daylight*, *Away With Words* and others. They're currently at work on a chapbook of lyric essays and auto-theory on the queer body.

Roisin Kiberd has written essays and features for the *New York Times*, the *Stinging Fly*, the *Dublin Review*, *Winter Papers*, the *White Review*, the *Guardian* and *Vice*, among others. Her first book, *The Disconnect*, was published by Serpent's Tail in 2021.

Lydia Hounat is a British-Algerian writer and photographer. Her work has appeared in *Hobart*, *Mai: Feminism & Visual Culture*, and the *Babel Tower Notice Board*. She edits interdisciplinary art zine, *Sober*, and is currently curating the French and Amazigh collections at Manchester Poetry Library.